Santa Clara County
LIBRARY

Renewals:
(800) 471-0991

The Pooh Bedside Reader

The Pooh Bedside Reader

In Which the Beloved Creations of A. A. Milne

and Ernest H. Shepard, Through Smackerels of

Verse, Amusing Excerpts, Anecdotes, Memoirs,

Reviews, and Autobiographies, Are Affectionately

Celebrated by **A. R. Melrose**

DUTTON BOOKS • NEW YORK

Library of Congress Cataloging-in-Publication Data

Melrose, A. R.
    The Pooh bedside reader / by A. R. Melrose.—1st edition
        p.   cm.
    "In which the beloved creations of A. A. Milne and Ernest H. Shepard, through smackerels of verse, amusing excerpts, anecdotes, memoirs, reviews, and autobiographies, are affectionately celebrated."
    ISBN 0-525-45600-7
    1. Milne, A. A. (Alan Alexander), 1882-1956—Characters—Winnie-the-Pooh. 2. Winnie-the-Pooh (Fictitious character)—Literary collections. 3. Children's literature, English—History and criticism. 4. Milne, A. A. (Alan Alexander), 1882-1956—Quotations. 5. Winnie-the-Pooh (Fictitious character) 6. Teddy bears in literature. 7. Animals in literature. 8. Toys in literature. I. Milne, A. A. (Alan Alexander), 1882-1956. II. Shepard, Ernest H. (Ernest Howard), 1879-1976. III. Title.
PR6025.I65Z77   1996
823'.912—dc20

96-34000
CIP

Published in the United States by Dutton Children's Books,
a division of Penguin Books USA Inc.
375 Hudson Street, New York, New York 10014

Designed by Lilian Rosenstreich
Printed in U.S.A.
First Edition
10 9 8 7 6 5 4 3 2

To Secret Code P.

Contents

Acknowledgments and Other Thanks

Eeyore was the one who said, "This writing business. Pencils and what-not. Over-rated, if you ask me. Silly stuff. Nothing in it." Yes, well, one could expect nothing less from someone who eats thistles all day. I have the following to thank for making the book possible and a great deal of fun: Audrey Griffiths, for typing most of the manuscript; Victoria Boyack and Justin Cargill, who—along with the staff of the Reference Department, Victoria University of Wellington—tracked down all requested material on Pooh; Louise Mason, who encouraged and helped me in any way she could; and Bob Mason, who child-minded.

I thank also the Trustees of the Pooh Properties, and especially the late Christopher Milne. I again enjoyed the support and wisdom of Joan Powers, Pooh Editor at Dutton Children's Books. My gratitude to her and to Christopher Franceschelli, Publisher.

The Pooh Bedside Reader

Introduction

Winnie-the-Pooh is a classic, some might argue a literary masterpiece. And this is the interesting thing (and this is the sort of Very Important Point I know Owl would like emphasized—at length if need be and with lots of big words): It is a classic because it is much loved. No one needs to be told to read it. What school library, public library, or bookshop is without a copy of *Winnie-the-Pooh*? A. A. Milne brilliantly wrote the book to be as pleasurable as possible to read. And the result has been a companion and friend to so many people in so many languages, editions, and sizes.

Of course, it might not so much be the book itself, but the Animals in it who deserve the attention. We have a bear given to eating and poetry, a donkey given to unhappiness and dour wit, a rabbit who is Captainish, and so on. Some Animals are wise and some wise in their own way—some are foolish and some very foolish. And some are bouncy (almost forgot Tigger). (And jumpy—thank you, Roo!)

In paying tribute to these Animals, we must start with the *toy* bear, Edward Bear, and then meet the *toy* pig, Piglet (who could fit nicely in a little boy's pocket), and on to the grey donkey whose stuffing sagged a little (well, quite a lot over the years), and other toys. And in trying to show what wonderful Animals they have become in *Winnie-the-Pooh,* we must realize that the real boy, Christopher Milne, had a nice sense of play, and his father had the magical gift of whimsical writing.

The real Pooh, the original Edward Bear, is now a Very Venerable Age (at least seventy-five years old!), and life's battles and cares are clearly to be seen on his face (you can see for yourself by visiting him at The New York Public Library). But *Winnie-the-Pooh,* the book about the Bear, is as fresh and delightful as the day it was written. And because other Pooh books have come along, and other Pooh stories have found their way into books and films, Winnie-the-Pooh, Piglet, Eeyore, Rabbit, Owl, Kanga, Roo, Tigger, and Christopher Robin are known and loved by more people than ever before.

The Pooh Bedside Reader is a celebration of these Animals in the form of a collection of character studies. We have brought together excerpts from the original books, early reviews and criticism, memoirs, newspaper reports, photographs, sketches, and the wonderful decorations of Ernest H. Shepard. As Piglet might explain it, this book is about Everyone being together in the Forest.

And us coming to visit . . .

Bear:
Winnie-the-Pooh

In which we are introduced to Pooh by Christopher Milne; are reminded of Pooh's names; his fondness for a little something or two; his fondness of Company (which may well be the same as having an Excuse for a Little Something to eat); his Lack of Brain; and his calling as a poet. We also have an article from The Times *(London) about a bear in a zoo called Winnie and where she came from, the stories Mr. Milne wrote about another bear called Winnie-the-Pooh and how successful these stories have become; and we have Letters (of Polite Disagreement) to the Editor of* The Times *(London) about the origins, the type, and the nature of the two Winnies . . .*

(. . . But we still don't know why Pooh lives under the name "Sanders.")

From Christopher Milne, *The Enchanted Places:*

A row of Teddy bears sitting in a toyshop, all one size, all one price. Yet how different each is from the next. Some look gay, some look sad. Some look stand-offish, some look lov-

5

The original Eeyore, Pooh, Kanga, Piglet, and Tigger, which are now on display at the Donnell Library in New York City

able. And one in particular, that one over there, has a specially endearing expression. Yes, that is the one we would like, please.

The bear took his place in the nursery and gradually he began to come to life. It started in the nursery; it started with me. It could really start nowhere else, for the toys lived in the nursery and they were mine and I played with them. And as I played with them and talked to them and gave them voices to answer with, so they began to breathe. But alone I couldn't take them very far. I needed help. So my mother joined me and she and I and the toys played together, and gradually more life, more character flowed into them, until they reached a point at which my father could take over.

Then, as the first stories were written, the cycle was repeated. The Pooh in my arms, the Pooh sitting opposite me at the breakfast table, was a Pooh who had climbed trees in search of honey, who had got stuck in a rabbit hole, who was "a bear of no brain at all." . . .

Then Shepard came along, looked at the toy Pooh, read the stories and started drawing; and the Pooh who had been developing under my father's pen began to develop under Shepard's pen as well. You will notice if you compare the early Poohs in *Winnie-the-Pooh* with the later Poohs in *The House At Pooh Corner*. What is it that gives Pooh his particularly Poohish look? It is the position of his eye. The eye that starts as quite an elaborate affair level with the top of Pooh's nose, gradually moves downwards and ends up as a mere dot level with his mouth. And in this dot the whole of Pooh's character can be read.

Pooh has character, and it is caught by the magic of the pencil. But why is he the Pooh? What is it about him that is so poohish? Remember "Cottleston Pie"? Mr. Milne once said that this was a song "which you sing when anybody says something you don't quite understand. You could say 'What?' or 'I beg your pardon,' but Pooh always used to sing 'Cottleston Pie.'"

> *Cottleston, Cottleston, Cottleston Pie.*
> *A fly can't bird, but a bird can fly.*
> *Ask me a riddle and I reply:*
> *"COTTLESTON, COTTLESTON, COTTLESTON PIE."*

Cottleston, Cottleston, Cottleston Pie.
A fish can't whistle and neither can I.
Ask me a riddle and I reply:
"COTTLESTON, COTTLESTON, COTTLESTON PIE."

Cottleston, Cottleston, Cottleston Pie.
Why does a chicken, I don't know why.
Ask me a riddle and I reply:
"COTTLESTON, COTTLESTON, COTTLESTON PIE."

Pooh hums: That is what he does and that is who he is. *Pooh is Full of Hums. And when he is not being a Friend of Piglet's, Eeyore's Comforter and Tail-finder, the Discoverer of the North Pole, and a Companion to Rabbit (as well as Tracker of Woozles, Wizzles, and the rarer Heffalump), Pooh is just waiting for a Good Hum to come to him. . . .*

From *The House At Pooh Corner:*

Before [Rabbit] had gone very far he heard a noise. So he stopped and listened. This was the noise.

NOISE, BY POOH

Oh, the butterflies are flying,
Now the winter days are dying,
And the primroses are trying
To be seen.

And the turtle-doves are cooing,
And the woods are up and doing,
For the violets are blue-ing
In the green.

Oh, the honey-bees are gumming
On their little wings, and humming
That the summer, which is coming
Will be fun.

And the cows are almost cooing,
And the turtle-doves are mooing,
Which is why a Pooh is poohing
In the sun.

For the spring is really springing;
You can see a skylark singing,
And the blue-bells, which are ringing,
Can be heard.

And the cuckoo isn't cooing,
But he's cucking and he's ooing,
And a Pooh is simply poohing
Like a bird.

"Hallo, Pooh," said Rabbit.

"Hallo, Rabbit," said Pooh dreamily.

"Did you make that song up?"

"Well, I sort of made it up," said Pooh. "It isn't Brain," he went on humbly, "because You Know Why, Rabbit; but it comes to me sometimes."

Pooh likes his HUNNY (and his Condensed Milk), and he likes Company in which to share in his eating. He might lack Brain, but he does well. He's a Friendly Sort of Bear. . . .

From *The House At Pooh Corner*:

"That it isn't," said Pooh.
"Isn't what?"
Pooh knew what he meant, but, being a Bear of Very Little Brain, couldn't think of the words.
"Well, it just isn't," he said again.

From *The House At Pooh Corner*:

An idea came to him.
"Owl," said Pooh, "I have thought of something."
"Astute and Helpful Bear," said Owl.
Pooh looked proud at being called a stout and helpful bear, and said modestly that he just happened to think of it.

From *Winnie-the-Pooh*:

EDWARD BEAR, known to his friends as Winnie-the-Pooh, or Pooh for short, was walking through the forest one day, humming proudly to himself. He had made up a little hum that very morning, as he was doing his Stoutness Exercises in front of the glass: *Tra-la-la, tra-la-la,* as he stretched up as high as he could go, and then *Tra-la-la, tra-la—oh, help!—la,* as he tried to reach his toes. After breakfast he had said it over and over to himself until he had learnt it off by heart, and now he was humming it right through, properly. It went like this:

> *Tra-la-la, tra-la-la,*
> *Tra-la-la, tra-la-la,*
> *Rum-tum-tiddle-um-tum.*
> *Tiddle-iddle, tiddle-iddle,*
> *Tiddle-iddle, tiddle-iddle,*
> *Rum-tum-tum-tiddle-um.*

Well, he was humming this hum to himself, and walking along gaily, wondering what everybody else was doing, and what it felt like, being somebody else, when suddenly he came to a sandy bank, and in the bank was a large hole.

"Aha!" said Pooh. *(Rum-tum-tiddle-um-tum.)* "If I know anything about anything, that hole means Rabbit," he said, "and Rabbit means Company," he said, "and Company means Food and Listening-to-Me-Humming and such like. *Rum-tum-tum-tiddle-um.*"

So he bent down, put his head into the hole, and called out: "Is anybody at home?"

There was a sudden scuffling noise from inside the hole, and then silence.

"What I said was, 'Is anybody at home?'" called out Pooh very loudly.

"No!" said a voice; and then added, "you needn't shout so loud. I heard you quite well the first time."

"Bother!" said Pooh. "Isn't there anybody here at all?"

"Nobody."

Winnie-the-Pooh took his head out of the hole, and thought for a little, and he thought to himself, "There must be somebody there, because somebody must have *said* 'Nobody.' " So he put his head back in the hole, and said:

"Hallo, Rabbit, isn't that you?"

"No," said Rabbit, in a different sort of voice this time.

"But isn't that Rabbit's voice?"

"I don't *think* so," said Rabbit. "It isn't *meant* to be."

"Oh!" said Pooh.

He took his head out of the hole, and had another think, and then he put it back, and said:

"Well, could you very kindly tell me where Rabbit is?"

"He has gone to see his friend Pooh Bear, who is a great friend of his."

"But this *is* Me!" said Bear, very much surprised.

"What sort of Me?"

"Pooh Bear."

"Are you sure?" said Rabbit, still more surprised.

"Quite, quite sure," said Pooh.

"Oh, well, then, come in."

So Pooh pushed and pushed and pushed his way through the hole, and at last he got in.

"You were quite right," said Rabbit, looking at him all over. "It *is* you. Glad to see you."

"Who did you think it was?"

"Well, I wasn't sure. You know how it is in the Forest. One can't have *anybody* coming into one's house. One has to be *careful*. What about a mouthful of something?"

Pooh always liked a little something at eleven o'clock in the morning, and he was very glad to see Rabbit getting out the plates and mugs; and when Rabbit said, "Honey or condensed milk with your bread?" he was so excited that he said, "Both," and then, so as not to seem greedy, he added, "but don't bother about the bread, please." And for a long time after that he said nothing . . . until at last, humming to himself in a rather sticky voice, he got up, shook Rabbit lovingly by the paw, and said that he must be going on.

"Must you?" said Rabbit politely.

"Well," said Pooh, "I could stay a little longer if it—if you—" and he tried very hard to look in the direction of the larder.

"As a matter of fact," said Rabbit, "I was going out myself directly."

"Oh, well, then, I'll be going on. Good-bye."

"Well, good-bye, if you're sure you won't have any more."

"*Is* there any more?" asked Pooh quickly.

Rabbit took the covers off the dishes, and said no, there wasn't.

"I thought not," said Pooh, nodding to himself. "Well, good-bye. I must be going on."

So he started to climb out of the hole. He pulled with his front paws, and pushed with his back paws, and in a little while his nose was out in the open again . . . and then his ears

. . . and then his front paws . . . and then his shoulders . . . and then—

"Oh, help!" said Pooh. "I'd better go back."

"Oh, bother!" said Pooh. "I shall have to go on."

"I can't do either!" said Pooh. "Oh, help *and* bother!"

Now by this time Rabbit wanted to go for a walk too, and finding the front door full, he went out by the back door, and came round to Pooh, and looked at him.

"Hallo, are you stuck?" he asked.

"N-no," said Pooh carelessly. "Just resting and thinking and humming to myself."

"Here, give us a paw."

Pooh Bear stretched out a paw, and Rabbit pulled and pulled and pulled. . . .

"*Ow!*" cried Pooh. "You're hurting!"

"The fact is," said Rabbit, "you're stuck."

"It all comes," said Pooh crossly, "of not having front doors big enough."

"It all comes," said Rabbit sternly, "of eating too much. I thought at the time," said Rabbit, "only I didn't like to say anything," said Rabbit, "that one of us was eating too much," said Rabbit, "and I knew it wasn't *me,*" he said.

Pooh *was originally the name given to a swan by Christopher Robin (1922 or so). "Because," writes Mr. A. A. Milne, "because, if you call him and he doesn't come (which is a thing swans are good at), then you can pretend that you were just saying 'Pooh!' to show how little you wanted him." And later, says Mr. Milne, "when we said good-bye, we took the name with us, as we didn't think the swan would want it any more." And so Edward Bear now has it—as well as the name "Winnie" from a real bear that once lived at London Zoo, and so he is Winnie-the-Pooh because . . . well, this is what the rest of this chapter is all about. (Among other things.)*

From *The Times* (London), January 31, 1981:

POOH, THE MOST ENGLISH TEDDY BEAR

It was customary for the Epilogue of the annual Latin play performed by the scholars of Westminster School to comment on current events. In 1897 the gold rush to the Yukon provided a target. "A gentleman gone to Klondyke" enters and is greeted as a polar bear: "Quis hic nunc advenit ursa polaris?" The gold rush polar bear was played by F. T. Barrington-Ward whose younger brother, also a scholar, became editor of *The Times*. In the audience each night or helping behind the scenes was another scholar, the 15-year-old A. A. Milne, whose own distinctive version of the polar bear struck it rich on a scale that most gold prospectors could only experience in their dreams.

Winnie was Christopher Robin's favourite polar bear at the London Zoo; Pooh was his toy swan. When his teddy bear, Edward, asked for a new and exciting name the solution was obvious. Winnie-the-Pooh has never looked back. . . .

In the 1970s the British edition alone sold half a million copies annually. But it is one of the fascinations of Milne's stories that this most English of Teddy Bears—bought at Harrods and brought up in Chelsea—has a world-wide appeal. The Pooh books were an immediate success in the United

States and have been translated into 23 languages including such improbable vehicles for teddy bear worship as Afrikaans, Japanese and Serbo-Croat. . . .

The secret of Pooh's appeal is intriguing. He is not a universal bear. With the exception of Japanese and Hebrew the modern languages into which he has been translated are those of countries—including the Soviet Union—whose history and culture have been shaped by Christianity. Pooh has failed to penetrate the Hindu and Moslem worlds. Is there an Arabic word for whimsical? But it appears to be relative affluence rather than religion that the Pooh countries have in common. They are countries where infant mortality is a thing of the past and where the development of the idea of childhood as a separate, defined stage of life associated with innocence and happiness created the conditions for the successful invasion of Pooh and his friends.

If that is right, then Pooh has many other conquests in store as more and more countries are able to afford the luxury of childhood. On the other hand the very affluence that created childhood may in time destroy it: television in particular is reducing the period of childhood and there are other forces, too, that operate on children like factory farming techniques, forcing them through the Pooh years so fast that the innocent world of the Hundred Acre wood may soon be squeezed out altogether.

Pooh's survival qualities are however remarkable. They include the expertise of Milne's writing and the brilliant simplicity of Ernest Shepard's illustrations. It is often forgotten that Milne was a journalist who had edited *Granta* at Cambridge and worked for eight years on *Punch*. The light touch and unforced humour are the marks of a professional, as is the absence of any message.

It is the besetting sin of writers of children's books that they feel they must have something to say as though simply writing for children was beneath their dignity. Milne never fell into that trap. But he almost made the mistake of rejecting Shepard as an illustrator. "What on earth do you see in that man?" he asked E. V. Lucas, the chairman of Methuen. "He's perfectly hopeless." Milne was wrong as he later acknowledged. The author from Westminster and the artist from St. Paul's complemented each other so perfectly that it is unthinkable that Pooh should appear in any other manifestation. . . . Together they created an ideal world, a cosy predictable paradise, "where springs not fail" and where—if Pooh can get his paws on it—there is always honey still for tea.

The original Pooh, up-market Harrodian bear, now lives in New York. He sits in a brightly-lit glass case in the reception room of his American publishers and is an object of pilgrimage for children from all over the United States. He comes back to England from time to time, travelling British Airways and using the VIP lounge in Kennedy and Heathrow airports. He is a celebrity. There is every hope that he will continue to be. His latest translation has been, appropriately, into Latin. Quis hic nunc advenit ursa polaris? Well, not exactly. Winnie-ille-Pu is Edwardus Ursus and *his* gold rush goes on and on.

JOHN RAE

The author is Head Master of Westminster School.

In 1987, the original Pooh Bear, along with Eeyore, Tigger, Piglet, and Kanga, were donated to the Donnell Branch of The New York Public Library. The toys are on display in a special climate-controlled case in the Central Children's Room.

LETTERS IN REPLY:

From Mr Rawle Knox (February 4, 1981):

Sir, The picture above Dr Rae's article (January 31) may well be that of Christopher Robin Milne's Winnie-the-Pooh, but it is not the bear from which Ernest Shepard made his original illustration, as stated in the caption.

That honour (recorded in my book, *The Work of E. H. Shepard*) goes to Growler, the teddy bear which belonged to the artist's son, Graham. Shepard called it "a magnificent bear." Growler was passed on to Graham's daughter, Minett (now Hunt), but perished during wartime exile in Canada, there worried to death by a dog.

> Yours faithfully,
> RAWLE KNOX,
> Fir Hill,
> Droxford, Hampshire.

From the Reverend Aubrey Moody (February 10, 1981):

Sir, Surely Mr John Rae is mistaken, in his article on January 31, in saying that "Winnie was Christopher Robin's favourite *polar* bear at the London Zoo." When I was a small boy, before *Winnie-the-Pooh* was written, I was taken as a treat behind the Mappin Terrace where a kindly keeper let a *brown* bear out into the long passage, and then pretended not to see as she made her way to a corn bin, opened the lid and stuck her head inside.

Pretending surprise, the keeper called her and she ambled back to us and gently opened my hand with her paw to get the lump of sugar that she knew would be there. Her name was Winnie and she had been the mascot of a Canadian regiment in the First World War.

Christopher Robin Milne at the London Zoo with his favorite bear, Winnie

Yours faithfully,
AUBREY MOODY,
Feering Vicarage,
Colchester, Essex.

From Mr Laurence Irving (February 14, 1981):

Sir, In your journal of record (January 31) your readers were gravely misled, albeit unwittingly, by Mr John Rae, the headmaster of Westminster School, on a matter of historical significance—namely the emergence of Pooh.

After the First World War, E. V. Lucas often invited me to accompany him to the Zoo. It was an outing not to be missed. For his friendships with the keepers opened to us the gates to a zoo within the zoo unknown to the general public. Our favourite inmate was a brown bear that had her den in the bowels of the Mappin Terraces where she received us and our proffered titbits with engaging courtesy. She had been the mascot of a Canadian regiment and had been left in the care of the Zoological Society. Her name was Winnie.

In 1926 a tuneful Scottish laird, Harold Fraser-Simpson, asked me to design the settings and costumes for a revue, *Vaudeville Vanities,* for which he had composed the music of two ballets, "A Venetian Wedding" and "The King's Breakfast." Among those who had contributed sketches and lyrics for this production were John Hastings Turner and Alan Milne; both were my friends and fellow members of the Garrick Club. Their children, Anne and "Billy" (Christopher Robin), respectively, were about the same age as our daughter Pamela. During the long run of the revue, to celebrate Pamela's fifth birthday, my wife and I invited Anne, Billy, and their mamas to join us in a visit to the zoo prior to a tea party in our home at Cumberland Terrace.

I had planned with a friendly keeper that the final *coup de théatre* of our expedition would be the presentation of the children to Winnie in her lair. In due course they followed our guide into the dark cavern leading to the iron grill of Winnie's cage. When he opened it Winnie, as was her custom, ambled out to greet our visitors. No doubt, in the narrow confines of the tunnel, to the children she appeared monstrous. The girls held their ground, Billy wavered, retreated a step or two, then overcame his awe and joined the girls in feeding and making much of the docile bear. Our guests declared that it had been a wonderful surprise.

The first hint I received of its historical consequences was from John Hastings Turner. With mischievous glee he described to me how at another party Billy's mother, Daphne, had recounted that confrontation and its endearing climax when her Billy had embraced Winnie as he sighed ecstatically: "Oh, Pooh!"

The rest is delightful nonsense.

> Yours etc,
> LAURENCE IRVING,
> The Lea, Wittersham,
> Kent.

From *Punch,* October 27, 1926:

I suppose Mr A. A. Milne has a sort of idea that Winnie-the-Pooh (Methuen) is partly his book and partly Mr E. H. Shepard's, theirs having been the actual hands (deft hands, I admit) that transcribed the adventures of the great Pooh and adorned them with unforgettable pictures. But, between ourselves, the book is *Christopher Robin's,* for whose sake and in whose society alone people like *Edward Bear, alias Sanders, alias Winnie-the-Pooh, Ee-yore* the donkey, *Piglet, Owl, Rabbit, Kanga* and *Baby Roo* take on character and immortality. These excellent people are even, I feel, a little embarrassed by Mr Milne. Only now and again, of course. The bits he puts in by himself—the pretty scenery in the story of *Ee-yore's* lost tail, for instance—are concessions to the drawing room. But to have captured so much of the tender ruthless nursery atmosphere shows reserves of a more primitive spirit; and the nursery, never slow to reward its skalds and *improvvisatori,* will acclaim and remember. They will remember *Winnie-the-Pooh,* a sort of *Tartarin* among bears, a little boastful but so bashful, a little greedy but so good-hearted, a little given to taking on enterprises that only luck can see him through, but so lucky. They will remember (with tears) the unfortunate *Ee-yore,* whose very thistles were sat on into saplessness by his less sensitive acquaintance. They will remember *Kanga,* proudest and most doctrinaire of parents, and the baby they stole from her (*Rabbit* and *Pooh*), and the terrible time she gave *Piglet,* carried off in her pouch instead. They will appreciate, without knowing why, the enchanting logicality and illogicality of the dialogue, and the consequent willingness of every grown-up person to read the whole book to them again and again.

Whatever reason for loving Pooh, and however illogical that reason may be, one thing is certain about Pooh: He *knows* what he *loves best—honey, Company, more honey, and honey preferably in Company. And Hums, of course.*

From *The House At Pooh Corner:*

... he said, "What I like best in the whole world is Me and Piglet going to see You, and You saying, 'What about a little something?' and Me saying, 'Well, I shouldn't mind a little something, should you, Piglet, and it being a hummy sort of day outside, and birds singing."

Boy: Christopher Robin

In which it is shown why Christopher Robin is so important to the stories of Pooh, and why he has two names; who Billy Moon might be; what the real Christopher thought about it all; and we have a complete story about the Christopher Robin who lives at the top of the Forest.

From *The House At Pooh Corner:*

"What are we going to do?" [Pooh] asked Piglet.

Piglet knew the answer to that, and he said at once that they must go and see Christopher Robin.

From A. A. Milne,
"The End of a Chapter" in *By Way of Introduction:*

To begin at the beginning: When Christopher Robin was born, he had to have a name. We had already decided to call him something else, and later on he decided to call himself something still else, so that the two names for which we were

now
looking were
to be no more than
an excuse for giving him
two initials for use in later
life. I had decided on two initials rather than one or none, because I
wanted him to play cricket for England,
like W. G. Grace and C. B. Fry, and if he was
to play as an amateur, two initials would give him
a more hopeful appearance on the score-card. A father has to
think of these things. So one of us liking the name Christopher, and the other maintaining that Robin was both pleasing
and unusual, we decided that as C. R. Milne he should be
encouraged to make his name in the sporting world.

'Christopher Robin,' then, he became on some legal docu-
ment, but as nobody ever called him so, we did not think any
more about it. However, three years later I wrote a book

called *When We Were Very Young,* and since he was much in my mind when I wrote it, I dedicated it to him. Now there is something about this book which I must explain; namely, that the adventures of a child as therein put down came from three sources.

    1. My memories of my own childhood.
    2. My imaginings of childhood in general.
    3. My observations of the particular
        childhood with which I was now in contact.

As a child I kept a mouse; probably it escaped—they generally do. Christopher Robin has kept almost everything except a mouse. As a child I played lines-and-squares in a casual sort of way. Christopher Robin never did until he read what I had written about it, and not very enthusiastically then. But he did go to Buckingham Palace a good deal (which I didn't) though not with Alice. And most children hop . . . and sometimes they sit half-way down the stairs—or, anyway, I can imagine them doing so . . . and Christopher Robin was very proud of his first pair of braces, though I never heard that he wanted a tail particularly. . . . And so on, and so on.

Well, now, you will have noticed that the words 'Christopher Robin' come very trippingly off the tongue. I noticed that too. You simply can't sit down to write verses for children, in a house with a child called (however officially only) Christopher Robin, without noticing it.

Christopher Robin goes
Hoppity hoppity—

Practically it writes itself.
But now consider:

Christopher Robin had
Great big
Waterproof
Boots on . . .

Hopeless. It simply must be John.

So it happened that into some of the verses the name Christopher Robin crept, and into some it didn't; and if you go through the book carefully, you will find that Christopher Robin is definitely associated with—how many do you think?—only three sets of verses. Three out of forty-four!

You can imagine my amazement and disgust, then, when I discovered that in a night, so to speak, I had been pushed into a back place, and that the hero of *When We Were Very Young* was not, as I had modestly expected, the author, but a curiously-named child of whom, at this time, I had scarcely heard. It was this Christopher Robin who kept mice, walked on the lines and not in the squares, and wondered what to do on a spring morning; it was this Christopher Robin, not I, whom Americans were clamouring to see; and, in fact (to make due acknowledgement at last), it was this Christopher Robin, not I, not the publishers, who was selling the book in such large and ridiculous quantities.

Now who was this Christopher Robin—the hero now, since it was so accepted, of *When We Were Very Young;* soon to be the hero of *Winnie-the-Pooh* and two other books? To me he was, and remained, the child of my imagination. When I thought of him, I thought of him in the Forest, living in his tree as no child really lives; not in the nursery, where a differently-named child (so far as we in this house are concerned) was playing with his animals. For this reason I have not felt self-conscious when writing about him, nor apologetic at the thought of exposing my own family to the public gaze.

The 'animals,' Pooh and Piglet, Eeyore, Kanga, and the rest, are in a different case. I have not 'created' them. He and his mother gave them life, and I have just 'put them into a

Christopher Robin and his mother, Daphne, in 1926

book.' You can see them now in the nursery, as Ernest Shepard saw them before he drew them. Between us, it may be, we have given them shape, but you have only to look at them to see, as I saw at once, that Pooh is a Bear of Very Little Brain, Tigger Bouncy, Eeyore Melancholy and so on. I have exploited them for my own profit, as I feel I have not exploited the legal Christopher Robin. All I have got from Christopher Robin is a name which he never uses, an introduction to his friends . . . and a gleam which I have tried to follow.

However, the distinction, if clear to me, is not so clear to others; and to them, anyhow, perhaps to me also, the dividing line between the imaginary and the legal Christopher Robin becomes fainter with each book. This, then, brings me (at last) to one of the reasons why these verses and stories have come to an end. I feel that the legal Christopher Robin has already had more publicity than I want for him. Moreover, since he is growing up, he will soon feel that he has had more publicity than he wants for himself. We all, young and old, hope to make some sort of a name, but we want to make it in our own chosen way, and, if possible, by our own exertions. To be the hero of the '3 not out' in that heroic finish between Oxford and Cambridge (Under Ten), to be undisputed Fluff Weight Champion (four stone six) of the Lower School, even to be the only boy of his age who can do Long Division: any of these is worth much more than all your vicarious literary reputations. Lawrence hid himself in the Air Force under the name of Shaw to avoid being introduced for the rest of his life as 'Lawrence of Arabia.' I do not want C. R. Milne ever to wish that his names were Charles Robert.

Christopher Robin Milne was born on August 21, 1920, and he became very famous as the boy in those *stories. Indeed, he became so famous that he could make the front page of* The New York Times. *(Note that his age is cited incorrectly.)*

From the front page of
The New York Times, March 19, 1928:

SON, 6, PLANS REVENGE POEMS ON MILNE WHEN HE GROWS UP

LONDON, March 18.—Christopher Robin, the boy immortalized by his father, A. A. Milne, for children the world over in "When We Were Very Young" and kindred volumes, plans, when he grows up, to take revenge upon his dad by writing poems about him.

The boy, who is now 6 years old, made his first public appearance yesterday in a Winnie the Pooh party given in aid of Queen Charlotte's Hospital. He sang "The Friend," one of his father's poems.

"It is fun being famous, but sometimes it is a nuisance," the boy told reporters. "Wait and see how father likes the poems I write about him."

The name of Christopher Robin was to haunt Christopher Milne most of his life. (Although it is probably just as true to say that Other People sought him out and haunted him because he had once *been Christopher Robin.) Christopher Milne grew up to be quite unlike* that *boy. When he died on April 20, 1996, Christopher Milne had lived a successful life as a husband, a fa-*

A. A. Milne and Christopher Robin in their London home

*ther, a bookseller, and a writer. He had married Lesley de Selin-
court after a courtship that involved "not love at first sight, but
rather a discovery that we liked doing things together. Particularly we liked doing nothing much together." And they had a
daughter, Clare, who was born with cerebral palsy.*

From Christopher Milne, *The Path Through the Trees:*

I have already mentioned the satisfaction I had found in designing and making furniture and equipment for Clare. And it did seem to me that, financed perhaps by those royalties I was so reluctant to accept for myself, this was something I might do for others. I might also convince myself that it was something Clare and I might do together. 'C. R. Milne & Daughter—Makers of Furniture for the Disabled.' The idea appealed to me: a pleasant dream.

From Christopher Milne, *The Enchanted Places:*

SELF PORTRAIT

HEIGHT: Small for his age.
WEIGHT: Underweight. Needs fattening up.

They did their best, of course, but it was really a waste of time, for no amount of eating has ever had any visible effect on me.

When I was a child I was what grown-ups describe as a fussy eater. That is to say I ate what I liked well enough, and as much of it as I could squeeze in; but what I didn't like I divided up into little bits and pushed around the plate and said "Need I, Nanny?" until she relented and I was allowed to leave it. I accepted that this was how it was with food, part pleasure, part penance. It never occurred to me that the penance part was unnecessary. I used to say that if ever I was sent to prison I would at least enjoy the meals, bread and water being what I was specially fond of. And I said this, not sadly, not complainingly, but almost with pride—a criticism of nursery food all the more telling for being quite unintended. . . .

So there I was, not eating enough and not nearly fat enough. Something had to be done, and, as I have said, they did their best. They tried strengthening medicine (which Tigger was so fond of). I was fond of it too, but it didn't make me any fatter. So then they tried gymnasium classes run by two Scotsmen called Munroe and Macpherson. On my first day, as we marched round the gym, horrible Mr. Macpherson shouted out: "Christopher Robin, you look like a camel. Hold yourself up, lad." But though I learnt to climb a rope, I still didn't get any fatter. So then they tried boxing classes. I cantered across the floor and struck Mr. Macpherson on the nose, and he pretended it was a fly tickling him and said: "Harder, lad, harder." But though I was very proud of my boxing gloves, my muscles didn't bulge the way they should. So then finally they tried massage. I lay on the ottoman in the nursery while Mrs. Preston powdered me and then thumped and kneaded. But though I loved it I remained resolutely underweight. And I have done so ever since.

APPEARANCE: Girlish.

Well, what can you expect? I had long hair at a time when boys didn't have long hair. One day Nanny went into the grocer's shop at the top of Oakley Street and left me lying outside in the pram. And while she was there two people came and peered at me and one of them said: "Oh, what a pretty little girl." That is not the sort of thing one forgets in a hurry. I used to wear girlish clothes, too, smocks and things. And in my very earliest dreams I even used to dream I was a girl.

GENERAL BEHAVIOUR: Very shy and un-self-possessed.

My father used to reassure me that he was shy too, that on the whole shy people were nicest, and that it was far better to be shy than boastful and self-assertive. But all the same I went a little too far the other way. When people asked me simple questions like did I want another piece of cake, I really ought to have known the answer and not turned to the hovering figure at my side and said, "Do I, Nanny?"

GENERAL INTELLIGENCE: Not very bright.

There was a story—I think it was Anne who told me, many years later—that Miss Walters from my kindergarten was so impressed by my dimness that she got herself invited to tea at Mallord Street to see whether I was always like that or only at school. I don't know what her

Christopher Robin with his nanny, Olive Rand, and Pooh. The Piglet in the foreground is not the original.

conclusions were. I don't know whether she came a little nearer to believing that I was not just being silly when I had said that I could do the difficult sums but not the easy ones.

GENERAL INTERESTS: Good with his hands.

Here at least was something I was all right at. I used to love making things. I sewed things (the Cottleston Pie that Pooh sang about was an egg cosy I made) and knitted things and made tapestry pictures. I had a Meccano set and made (among other things) a working grandfather clock. Or rather I made the works and a friend, older than I, came to tea one day and helped me with the case, the weights and the pendulum. That night, however, I couldn't get to sleep. I lay awake all restless and unhappy. Finally, I called out:

"Nanny, can you come?"

"What is it, dear?"

"It's the clock. I don't want to keep it. You see I didn't do it all myself. Alec helped me with it. So can you take it to bits, please: just the stand part. Can you start doing it now?"

So she did: one of the odder things that Nannies get called upon to do. Then there were the things that I took to bits myself. Using a penknife, I once took a dead mouse to bits to see how it worked. But it was hard to tell exactly and really rather disappointing and so I threw it away. I also took the lock on the night nursery door to bits. I discovered how it worked but not how it went together again. So an ironmonger had to be summoned. What! Couldn't my father have mended it? My *father,* did you say? *Mend* something? Even at the age of seven I was already the family's Chief Mender. And mostly I succeeded. Admittedly the lock was a failure, and another failure was when I tried to run my 6 volt electric motor by connecting it up to the electric light switch. Nothing happened. Even now, looking back on the event with greater electrical knowledge, I still can't understand why *nothing* happened.

It will now, I hope, be apparent . . . that the poem "The Engineer" was not about me. The poem begins:

Let it rain
Who cares
I've a train
Upstairs
With a brake
Which I make . . .

and it ends up:

It's a good sort of brake
But it hasn't worked yet.

I may have been a bit undersize. I may have been a bit underweight. I may have looked like a girl. I may have been shy. I may have been on the dim side. But if I'd had a train (and I didn't have a train) any brake that I'd wanted to make for it—any simple thing like a brake—WOULD HAVE WORKED.

Christopher Robin, who lived at the top of the Forest, may have dressed in a smock, but to all the Animals (especially Piglet) he was one who knew the Thing to Do. There can be no arguing

Christopher Robin and Pooh in the boy's favorite place—the hollow walnut tree at Cotchford Farm

that Pooh is everybody's favorite (although I have met some people who think Piglet *is the* best *character of the books, and then there are some who might argue that* Eeyore *makes the books worthwhile, and not forgetting one woman I know who positively admires* Rabbit*). Anyway, of everyone mentioned in the*

Pooh stories, it is Christopher Robin who is the PIVOTAL char-
acter. He is first introduced to us as the boy to whom the stories
are told, and then he becomes the boy in *the stories. Finally, he is*
the one to whom the Forest Animals turn for leadership (sorry,
Rabbit) and safety. Christopher Robin always Sorts Things Out,
and he Knows When Things Have Happened.

From *Winnie-the-Pooh:*

CHRISTOPHER ROBIN LEADS AN EXPOTITION
TO THE NORTH POLE

One fine day Pooh had stumped up to the top of the Forest to
see if his friend Christopher Robin was interested in Bears at
all. At breakfast that morning (a simple meal of marmalade
spread lightly over a honeycomb or two) he had suddenly
thought of a new song. It began like this:

"Sing Ho! for the life of a Bear!"

When he had got as far as this, he stretched his head, and
thought to himself, "That's a very good start for a song, but
what about the second line?" He tried singing "Ho," two or
three times, but it didn't seem to help. "Perhaps it would be
better," he thought, "if I sang Hi for the life of a Bear." So he
sang it . . . but it wasn't. "Very well, then," he said, "I shall
sing that first line twice, and perhaps if I sing it very quickly,
I shall find myself singing the third and fourth lines before I
have time to think of them, and that will be a Good Song.
Now then:"

Sing Ho! for the life of a Bear!
Sing Ho! for the life of a Bear!
I don't much mind if it rains or snows,
'Cos I've got a lot of honey on my nice new nose,
I don't much care if it snows or thaws,
'Cos I've got a lot of honey on my nice clean paws!
Sing Ho! for a Bear!
Sing Ho! for a Pooh!
And I'll have a little something in an hour or two!

He was so pleased with this song that he sang it all the way to the top of the Forest, "and if I go on singing it much longer," he thought, "it will be time for the little something, and then the last line won't be true." So he turned it into a hum instead.

Christopher Robin was sitting outside his door, putting on his Big Boots. As soon as he saw the Big Boots, Pooh knew that an Adventure was going to happen, and he brushed the honey off his nose with the back of his paw, and spruced himself up as well as he could, so as to look Ready for Anything.

"Good-morning, Christopher Robin," he called out.

"Hallo, Pooh Bear. I can't get this boot on."

"That's bad," said Pooh.

"Do you think you could very kindly lean against me, 'cos I keep pulling so hard that I fall over backwards."

Pooh sat down, dug his feet into the ground, and pushed hard against Christopher Robin's back, and Christopher Robin pushed hard against his, and pulled and pulled at his boot until he had got it on.

"And that's that," said Pooh. "What do we do next?"

"We are all going on an Expedition," said Christopher Robin, as he got up and brushed himself. "Thank you, Pooh."

"Going on an Expotition?" said Pooh eagerly. "I don't think I've ever been on one of those. Where are we going to on this Expotition?"

"Expedition, silly old Bear. It's got an 'x' in it."

"Oh!" said Pooh. "I know." But he didn't really.

"We're going to discover the North Pole."

"Oh!" said Pooh again. "What *is* the North Pole?" he asked.

"It's just a thing you discover," said Christopher Robin carelessly, not being quite sure himself.

"Oh! I see," said Pooh. "Are bears any good at discovering it?"

"Of course they are. And Rabbit and Kanga and all of you. It's an Expedition. That's what an Expedition means. A long line of everybody. You'd better tell the others to get ready, while I see if my gun's all right. And we must all bring Provisions."

"Bring what?"

"Things to eat."

"Oh!" said Pooh happily. "I thought you said Provisions. I'll go and tell them." And he stumped off.

The first person he met was Rabbit.

"Hallo, Rabbit," he said, "is that you?"

"Let's pretend it isn't," said Rabbit, "and see what happens."

"I've got a message for you."

"I'll give it to him."

"We're all going on an Expotition with Christopher Robin!"

"What is it when we're on it?"

"A sort of boat, I think," said Pooh.

"Oh! that sort."

"Yes. And we're going to discover a Pole or something. Or was it a Mole? Anyhow we're going to discover it."

"We are, are we?" said Rabbit.

"Yes. And we've got to bring Po-things to eat with us. In case we want to eat them. Now I'm going down to Piglet's. Tell Kanga, will you?"

He left Rabbit and hurried down to Piglet's house. The Piglet was sitting on the ground at the door of his house blowing happily at a dandelion, and wondering whether it would be this year, next year, sometime or never. He had just discovered that it would be never, and was trying to remember what *"it"* was, and hoping it wasn't anything nice, when Pooh came up.

"Oh! Piglet," said Pooh excitedly, "we're going on an Expotition, all of us, with things to eat. To discover something."

"To discover what?" said Piglet anxiously.

"Oh! just something."

"Nothing fierce?"

"Christopher Robin didn't say anything about fierce. He just said it had an 'x'."

"It isn't their necks I mind," said Piglet earnestly. "It's their teeth. But if Christopher Robin is coming I don't mind anything."

In a little while they were all ready at the top of the Forest, and the Expotition started. First came Christopher Robin and Rabbit, then Piglet and Pooh; then Kanga, with Roo in her pocket, and Owl; then Eeyore; and, at the end, in a long line, all Rabbit's friends-and-relations.

"I didn't ask them," explained Rabbit carelessly. "They just came. They always do. They can march at the end, after Eeyore."

"What I say," said Eeyore, "is that it's unsettling. I didn't want to come on this Expo—what Pooh said. I only came to oblige. But here I am; and if I am the end of the Expo—what we're talking about—then let me *be* the end. But if, every time I want to sit down for a little rest, I have to brush away half a dozen of Rabbit's smaller friends-and-relations first, then this isn't an Expo—whatever it is—at all, it's simply a Confused Noise. That's what *I* say."

"I see what Eeyore means," said Owl. "If you ask me—"

"I'm not asking anybody," said Eeyore. "I'm just telling everybody. We can look for the North Pole, or we can play 'Here we go gathering Nuts and May' with the end part of an ant's nest. It's all the same to me."

There was a shout from the top of the line.

"Come on!" called Christopher Robin.

"Come on!" called Pooh and Piglet.

"Come on!" called Owl.

"We're starting," said Rabbit. "I must go." And he hurried off to the front of the Expotition with Christopher Robin.

"All right," said Eeyore. "We're going. Only Don't Blame Me."

So off they all went to discover the Pole. And as they walked, they chattered to each other of this and that, all except Pooh, who was making up a song.

"This is the first verse," he said to Piglet, when he was ready with it.

"First verse of what?"

"My song."

"What song?"

"This one."

"Which one?"

"Well, if you listen, Piglet, you'll hear it."

"How do you know I'm not listening?"

Pooh couldn't answer that one, so he began to sing.

> *They all went off to discover the Pole,*
> *Owl and Piglet and Rabbit and all;*
> *It's a Thing you Discover, as I've been tole*
> *By Owl and Piglet and Rabbit and all.*
> *Eeyore, Christopher Robin and Pooh*
> *And Rabbit's relations all went too ——*
> *And where the Pole was none of them knew. . . .*
> *Sing Hey! for Owl and Rabbit and all!*

"Hush!" said Christopher Robin turning round to Pooh, "we're just coming to a Dangerous Place."

"Hush!" said Pooh turning round quickly to Piglet.

"Hush!" said Piglet to Kanga.

"Hush!" said Kanga to Owl, while Roo said "Hush!" several times to himself very quietly.

"Hush!" said Owl to Eeyore.

"Hush!" said Eeyore in a terrible voice to all Rabbit's friends-and-relations, and "Hush!" they said hastily to each other all down the line, until it got to the last one of all. And the last and smallest friend-and-relation was so upset to find that the whole Expotition was saying "Hush!" to *him,* that he buried himself head downwards in a crack in the ground, and stayed there for two days until the danger was over, and then went home in a great hurry, and lived quietly with his Aunt ever-afterwards. His name was Alexander Beetle.

They had come to a stream which twisted and tumbled between high rocky banks, and Christopher Robin saw at once how dangerous it was.

"It's just the place," he explained, "for an Ambush."

"What sort of bush?" whispered Pooh to Piglet. "A gorse-bush?"

"My dear Pooh," said Owl in his superior way, "don't you know what an Ambush is?"

"Owl," said Piglet, looking round at him severely, "Pooh's whisper was a perfectly private whisper, and there was no need—"

"An Ambush," said Owl, "is a sort of Surprise."

"So is a gorse-bush sometimes," said Pooh.

"An Ambush, as I was about to explain to Pooh," said Piglet, "is a sort of Surprise."

"If people jump out at you suddenly, that's an Ambush," said Owl.

"It's an Ambush, Pooh, when people jump out at you suddenly," explained Piglet.

Pooh, who now knew what an Ambush was, said that a gorse-bush had sprung at him suddenly one day when he fell off a tree, and he had taken six days to get all the prickles out of himself.

"We are not *talking* about gorse-bushes," said Owl a little crossly.

"I am," said Pooh.

They were climbing very cautiously up the stream now, going from rock to rock, and after they had gone a little way they came to a place where the banks widened out at each side, so that on each side of the water there was a level strip of grass on which they could sit down and rest. As soon as he saw this, Christopher Robin called "Halt!" and they all sat down and rested.

"I think," said Christopher Robin, "that we ought to eat all our Provisions now, so that we shan't have so much to carry."

"Eat all our what?" said Pooh.

"All that we've brought," said Piglet, getting to work.

"That's a good idea," said Pooh, and he got to work too.

"Have you all got something?" asked Christopher Robin with his mouth full.

"All except me," said Eeyore. "As Usual." He looked round at them in his melancholy way. "I suppose none of you are sitting on a thistle by any chance?"

"I believe I am," said Pooh. "Ow!" He got up, and looked behind him. "Yes, I was. I thought so."

"Thank you, Pooh. If you've quite finished with it." He moved across to Pooh's place, and began to eat.

"It don't do them any Good, you know, sitting on them," he went on, as he looked up munching. "Takes all the Life out of them. Remember that another time, all of you. A little Consideration, a little Thought for Others, makes all the difference."

As soon as he had finished his lunch Christopher Robin whispered to Rabbit, and Rabbit said, "Yes, yes, of course," and they walked a little way up the stream together.

"I didn't want the others to hear," said Christopher Robin.

"Quite so," said Rabbit, looking important.

"It's—I wondered—It's only—Rabbit, I suppose *you* don't know, What does the North Pole *look* like."

"Well," said Rabbit, stroking his whiskers. "Now you're asking me."

"I did know once, only I've sort of forgotten," said Christopher Robin carelessly.

"It's a funny thing," said Rabbit, "but I've sort of forgotten too, although I did know *once*."

"I suppose it's just a pole stuck in the ground?"

"Sure to be a pole," said Rabbit, "because of calling a pole, and if it's a pole, well, I should think it would be sticking in the ground, shouldn't you, because there'd be nowhere else to stick it."

"Yes, that's what I thought."

"The only thing," said Rabbit, "is, *where is it sticking?*"

"That's what we're looking for," said Christopher Robin.

They went back to the others. Piglet was lying on his back, sleeping peacefully. Roo was washing his face and paws in the stream, while Kanga explained to everybody proudly that this was the first time he had ever washed his face himself, and Owl was telling Kanga an Interesting Anecdote full of long words like Encyclopaedia and Rhododendron to which Kanga wasn't listening.

"I don't hold with all this washing," grumbled Eeyore. "This modern Behind-the-ears nonsense. What do *you* think, Pooh?"

"Well," said Pooh, "*I* think—"

But we shall never know what Pooh thought, for there came a sudden squeak from Roo, a splash, and a loud cry of alarm from Kanga.

"So much for *washing*," said Eeyore.

"Roo's fallen in!" cried Rabbit, and he and Christopher Robin came rushing down to the rescue.

"Look at me swimming!" squeaked Roo from the middle of his pool, and was hurried down a waterfall into the next pool.

"Are you all right, Roo dear?" called Kanga anxiously.

"Yes!" said Roo. "Look at me sw—" and down he went over the next waterfall into another pool.

Everybody was doing something to help. Piglet, wide

awake suddenly, was jumping up and down and making "Oo, I say" noises; Owl was explaining that in a case of Sudden and Temporary Immersion the Important Thing was to keep the Head Above Water; Kanga was jumping along the bank, saying "Are you *sure* you're all right, Roo dear?" to which Roo, from whatever pool he was in at the moment, was answering "Look at me swimming!" Eeyore had turned round and hung his tail over the first pool into which Roo fell, and with his back to the accident was grumbling quietly to himself, and saying, "All this washing; but catch on to my tail, little Roo, and you'll be all right"; and Christopher Robin and Rabbit came hurrying past Eeyore, and were calling out to the others in front of them.

"All right, Roo, I'm coming," called Christopher Robin.

"Get something across the stream lower down, some of you fellows," called Rabbit.

But Pooh was getting something. Two pools below Roo he was standing with a long pole in his paws, and Kanga came up and took one end of it, and between them they held it across the lower part of the pool; and Roo, still bubbling proudly, "Look at me swimming," drifted up against it, and climbed out.

"Did you see me swimming?" squeaked Roo excitedly, while Kanga scolded him and rubbed him down. "Pooh, did you see me swimming? That's called swimming, what I was doing. Rabbit, did you see what I was doing? Swimming. Hallo, Piglet! I say, Piglet! What do you think I was doing! Swimming! Christopher Robin, did you see me—"

But Christopher Robin wasn't listening. He was looking at Pooh.

"Pooh," he said, "where did you find that pole?"

Pooh looked at the pole in his hands.

"I just found it," he said. "I thought it ought to be useful. I just picked it up."

"Pooh," said Christopher Robin solemnly, "the Expedition is over. You have found the North Pole!"

"Oh!" said Pooh.

Eeyore was sitting with his tail in the water when they all got back to him.

"Tell Roo to be quick, somebody," he said. "My tail's getting cold. I don't want to mention it, but I just mention it. I don't want to complain but there it is. My tail's cold."

"Here I am!" squeaked Roo.

"Oh, there you are."

"Did you see me swimming?"

Eeyore took his tail out of the water, and swished it from side to side.

"As I expected," he said. "Lost all feeling. Numbed it. That's what it's done. Numbed it. Well, as long as nobody minds, I suppose it's all right."

"Poor old Eeyore. I'll dry it for you," said Christopher Robin, and he took out his handkerchief and rubbed it up.

"Thank you, Christopher Robin. You're the only one who seems to understand about tails. They don't think—that's what's the matter with some of these others. They've no imagination. A tail isn't a tail to *them,* it's just a Little Bit Extra at the back."

"Never mind, Eeyore," said Christopher Robin, rubbing his hardest. "Is *that* better?"

"It's feeling more like a tail perhaps. It Belongs again, if you know what I mean."

"Hullo, Eeyore," said Pooh, coming up to them with his pole.

"Hullo, Pooh. Thank you for asking, but I shall be able to use it again in a day or two."

"Use what?" said Pooh.

"What we are talking about."

"I wasn't talking about anything," said Pooh, looking puzzled.

"My mistake again. I thought you were saying how sorry you were about my tail, being all numb, and could you do anything to help?"

"No," said Pooh. "That wasn't me," he said. He thought for a little and then suggested helpfully, "Perhaps it was somebody else."

"Well, thank him for me when you see him."

Pooh looked anxiously at Christopher Robin.

"Pooh's found the North Pole," said Christopher Robin. "Isn't that lovely?"

Pooh looked modestly down.

"Is that it?" said Eeyore.

"Yes," said Christopher Robin.

"Is that what we were looking for?"

"Yes," said Pooh.

"Oh!" said Eeyore. "Well, anyhow—it didn't rain," he said.

They stuck the pole in the ground, and Christopher Robin tied a message on to it.

NORTH POLE

DICSOVERED BY POOH

POOH FOUND IT.

Then they all went home again.
And I think, but I am not quite sure,
that Roo had a hot bath and went
straight to bed. But Pooh
went back to his own
house, and feeling very
proud of what he had
done, had a little some-
thing to revive himself.

Educated and Speling Animals: Rabbit and WOL

In which we get told again that Rabbit and Owl can think; that Rabbit has Brain; that Rabbit is a Very Important Animal; and that Owl knows Speling.

Pooh, Eeyore, and Piglet were the original toys around which Winnie-the-Pooh *and later* The House At Pooh Corner *grew, but as the stories developed, more characters were needed and so new characters were invented. For this reason, Rabbit and Owl were never toys. They were Rabbit and Owl from the moment Mr. Milne wrote their names. As Christopher Milne puts it: "Owl was owlish from the start and always remained so. But Rabbit, I suspect, began by being just the owner of the hole in which Pooh got stuck and then, as the stories went on, became less rabbity and more Rabbity; for rabbits are not by nature good organizers."*

Mr. Milne must have enjoyed Rabbit, who, once he appears, appears again and again. He is a Captainish Animal, Good at Everything Important (like Thinking, Spelling, Organizing).

53

And most of all, Rabbit looks after his friends (of which he has many).

From *The House At Pooh Corner:*

It was going to be one of Rabbit's busy days. As soon as he woke up he felt important, as if everything depended upon him. It was just the day for Organizing Something, or for Writing a Notice Signed Rabbit, or for Seeing What Everybody Else Thought About It. It was a perfect morning for hurrying round to Pooh, and saying, "Very well, then, I'll tell Piglet," and then going to Piglet, and saying, "Pooh thinks—but perhaps I'd better see Owl first." It was a Captainish sort of day, when everybody said, "Yes, Rabbit" and "No, Rabbit," and waited until he had told them.

He came out of his house and sniffed the warm spring morning as he wondered what he would do. Kanga's house was nearest, and at Kanga's house was Roo, who said "Yes, Rabbit" and "No, Rabbit" almost better than anybody else in the Forest; but there was another animal there nowadays, the strange and Bouncy Tigger; and he was the sort of Tigger who was always in front when you were showing him the way anywhere, and was generally out of sight when at last you came to the place and said proudly, "Here we are!"

"No, not Kanga's," said Rabbit thoughtfully to himself, as

he curled his whiskers in the sun; and, to make quite sure that he wasn't going there, he turned to the left and trotted off in the other direction, which was the way to Christopher Robin's house.

"After all," said Rabbit to himself, "Christopher Robin depends on Me. He's fond of Pooh and Piglet and Eeyore, and so am I, but they haven't any Brain. Not to notice. And he respects Owl, because you can't help respecting anybody who can spell TUESDAY, even if he doesn't spell it right; but spelling isn't everything. There are days when spelling Tuesday simply doesn't count. And Kanga is too busy looking after Roo, and Roo is too young and Tigger is too bouncy to be any help, so there's really nobody but Me, when you come to look at it."

Rabbit and Owl are friends because they share a common gift: Brains. (And of all the Animals these two have the most relations—Rabbit has many; Owl has two.) Yet they are such different Animals. . . .

From *The House At Pooh Corner:*

"Owl," said Rabbit shortly, "you and I have brains. The others have fluff. If there is any thinking to be done in this Forest—and when I say thinking I mean *thinking*—you and I must do it."

"Yes," said Owl. "I was."

"Read that."

Owl took Christopher Robin's notice from Rabbit and looked at it nervously. He could spell his own name WOL, and he could spell Tuesday so that you knew it wasn't Wednesday, and he could read quite comfortably when you weren't looking over his shoulder and saying "Well?" all the time, and he could—

"Well?" said Rabbit.

"Yes," said Owl, looking Wise and Thoughtful. "I see what you mean. Undoubtedly."

"Well?"

"Exactly," said Owl. "Precisely." And he added, after a little thought, "If you had not come to me, I should have come to you."

From *The House At Pooh Corner:*

"We've come to wish you a Very Happy Thursday," said Pooh, when he had gone in and out once or twice just to make sure he *could* get out again.

"Why, what's going to happen on Thursday?" asked Rabbit, and when Pooh had explained, and Rabbit, whose life was made up of Important Things, said, "Oh, I thought you'd really come about something," they sat down for a little . . . and by-and-by Pooh and Piglet went on again. The wind was behind them now, so they didn't have to shout.

"Rabbit's clever," said Pooh thoughtfully.

"Yes," said Piglet, "Rabbit's clever."

"And he has Brain."

"Yes," said Piglet, "Rabbit has Brain."

There was a long silence.

"I suppose," said Pooh, "that that's why he never understands anything."

From *Winnie-the-Pooh:*

"There's Pooh," [Piglet] thought to himself. "Pooh hasn't much Brain, but he never comes to any harm. He does silly things and they turn out right. There's Owl. Owl hasn't exactly got Brain, but he Knows Things. . . . There's Rabbit. He hasn't Learnt in Books, but he can always Think of a Clever Plan."

Rabbit always has a Plan. Very little happens in the Forest without Rabbit. It is Rabbit to whom Christopher Robin turns when the Expotition loses its way. Rabbit organdizes the Hunt for Small. And devises a Plan to Get Rid of Kanga (and Roo). And has the Plan to Teach Tigger a Lesson.

These Plans do become a little complicated. Some might say very complicated. In fact, if someone cared to spend some hard thinking time (and, to many animals, thinking is hard), a Plan *of what really always happens might be made up. . . .*

From Frederick C. Crews,
The Pooh Perplex, A Freshman Casebook:

A COMPLETE ANALYSIS OF *WINNIE-THE-POOH,*
BY DUNS C. PENWIPER

If we let A stand for one of the characters, B for a second, and C (following out the established pattern of consecutive form) for a third, we see that there are various situations in *Winnie-the-Pooh* employing some of the most complicated devices of plot known to criticism. A's relationship to B is often such that C, who had hoped to establish a certain contact with B, finds himself constrained instead to deal with A. Or again, C may initiate an action against A; A replies by appealing to B; B thinks over the matter to himself, decides not to act, and departs; C and A are thus left on the scene to resolve their differences, either by C's reconciling himself to A, A's reconciling himself to C, or A's (or C's) undertaking a decisive finishing action *against* the other. Still more intricate are the plot situations in which A, B, and C have nothing whatever to say to each other, but are obliged to remain together on barely amicable terms until the end of the episode. This we call the "Jamesian" situation, which draws its complexity from the subtleties of appeal, criticism, muted disrespect, and barbed repartee among the characters involved. And to finish our survey, we must not omit the type of situation in which A, B, and C, preoccupied by a common problem, set off together and are joined by D, E, and F (standing for further characters in the plot); G, H, and I then arrive, accompanied by J, K, and L. Soon, in the company of M, N, and O, the other characters set off to discover either a particular object or place, or the further characters P, Q, and R; and when this has been successfully done the entire group, from A through R, sits down to a hearty lunch.

And where do these As and Bs and Ps and Os come from? This is where Rabbit comes into his own, and also why he is such a good organizer. You can't organize without someones *to organize, and Rabbit knows lots of people—of course, he does—because this is what a rabbit always does best—have lots of friends-and-relations!*

In Mr. Shepard's decoration showing Pooh's Special Party there are at least eighteen friends-and-relations hanging about the table (waiting "hopefully in case anybody spoke to them, or dropped anything, or asked them the time"), and in the picture of Pooh stuck in Rabbit's hole, there are fifteen friends-and-relations (not counting Piglet and Christopher Robin) trying to get him out.

LIST OF RABBIT'S FRIENDS-AND-RELATIONS
hedgehogs
the Beetle Family, including Henry Rush
Alexander Beetle (and his Aunt, but we are not
told whether she is a friend or a relation)
Smallest-of-All (also known as S. of A.)
Late
Early
Small (another Beetle)
the other numerous F's and R's of "such different sorts and sizes," including the one who left a blue balloon behind at a party, "being really too young to go to a party at all."

And Owl has relations too: "an aunt who had laid a seagull's egg by mistake," and Uncle Robert, whose portrait hung upon the

wall. (This uncle is not to be confused with the uncle of Pooh's who claims to have once seen cheese the color of honey.) And Owl is Special. He not only Knows Things and can Explain Things (however long it takes to do so), but he also has the Necessary Dorsal Muscles so that he can fly. Flying is a strange business: Not only is flying that Special Thing that Owl can do (and likes to do), but Owl can even do that Special Thing called Spelling. He likes that too. Or has that already been mentioned?

From *Winnie-the-Pooh:*

Pooh looked after [Kanga] as she went.

"I wish I could jump like that," he thought. "Some can and some can't. That's how it is."

But there were moments when Piglet wished that Kanga couldn't. Often when he had had a long walk home through the Forest, he had wished that he were a bird; but now he thought jerkily to himself at the bottom of Kanga's pocket, this   take

"If   is   shall   really   to

flying   I   never   it."

And as he went up in the air he said, *"Ooooooo!"* and as he came down he said *"Ow!"* And he was saying *"Ooooooo-ow, Ooooooo-ow, Ooooooo-ow"* all the way to Kanga's house.

From *The House At Pooh Corner:*

"Could you fly up to the letter-box with Piglet on your back?" Pooh asked Owl.

"No," said Piglet quickly. "He couldn't."

Owl explained about the Necessary Dorsal Muscles. He had explained this to Pooh and Christopher Robin once before, and had been waiting ever since for a chance to do it again, because it is a thing which you can easily explain twice before anybody knows what you are talking about.

From *Winnie-the-Pooh:*

"And if anyone knows anything about anything," said Bear to himself, "it's Owl who knows something about something," he said, "or my name's not Winnie-the-Pooh," he said. "Which it is," he added. "So there you are."

Owl lived at The Chestnuts, an old-world residence of great charm, which was grander than anybody else's, or seemed so to Bear, because it had both a knocker *and* a bell-pull. Underneath the knocker there was a notice which said:

PLES RING IF AN RNSER IS REQIRD.

Underneath the bell-pull there was a notice which said:

PLEZ CNOKE IF AN RNSR IS NOT REQID.

These notices had been written by Christopher Robin, who was the only one in the forest who could spell; for Owl, wise though he was in many ways, able to read and write and spell his own name WOL, yet somehow went all to pieces

over delicate words like MEASLES and BUTTERED TOAST.

Winnie-the-Pooh read the two notices very carefully, first from left to right, and afterwards, in case he had missed some of it, from right to left. Then, to make quite sure, he knocked and pulled the knocker, and he pulled and knocked the bell-rope, and he called out in a very loud voice, "Owl! I require an answer! It's Bear speaking." And the door opened, and Owl looked out.

"Hallo, Pooh," he said. "How's things?"

"Terrible and Sad," said Pooh, "because Eeyore, who is a friend of mine, has lost his tail. And he's Moping about it. So could you very kindly tell me how to find it for him?"

"Well," said Owl, "the customary procedure in such cases is as follows."

"What does Crustimoney Proseedcake mean?" said Pooh. "For I am a Bear of Very Little Brain, and long words Bother me."

"It means the Thing to Do."

"As long as it means that, I don't mind," said Pooh humbly.

"The thing to do is as follows. First, Issue a Reward. Then—"

"Just a moment," said Pooh, holding up his paw. "*What* do we do to this—what you were saying? You sneezed just as you were going to tell me."

"I *didn't* sneeze."

"Yes, you did, Owl."

"Excuse me, Pooh, I didn't. You can't sneeze without knowing it."

"Well, you can't know it without something having been sneezed."

"What I *said* was, 'First *Issue* a Reward.' "

"You're doing it again," said Pooh sadly.

"A Reward!" said Owl very loudly. "We write a notice to say that we will give a large something to anybody who finds Eeyore's tail."

"I see, I see," said Pooh, nodding his head. "Talking about large somethings," he went on dreamily, "I generally have a small something about now—about this time in the morning," and he looked wistfully at the cupboard in the corner of Owl's parlour; "just a mouthful of condensed milk or what not, with perhaps a lick of honey—"

"Well, then," said Owl, "we write out this notice, and we put it up all over the forest."

"A lick of honey," murmured Bear to himself, "or—or not, as the case may be."

And he gave a deep sigh, and tried very hard to listen to what Owl was saying.

But Owl went on and on, using longer and longer words, until at last he came back to where he started, and he explained that the person to write out this notice was Christopher Robin.

From *Winnie-the-Pooh:*

"Good morning, Pooh," said Owl.

"Many happy returns of Eeyore's birthday," said Pooh.

"Oh, is that what it is?"

"What are you giving him, Owl?"

"What are *you* giving him, Pooh?"

"I'm giving him a Useful Pot to Keep Things In, and I wanted to ask you—"

"Is this it?" said Owl, taking it out of Pooh's paw.

"Yes, and I wanted to ask you—"

"Somebody has been keeping honey in it," said Owl.

"You can keep *anything* in it," said Pooh earnestly. "It's Very Useful like that. And I wanted to ask you—"

"You ought to write 'A Happy Birthday' on it."

"*That* was what I wanted to ask you," said Pooh. "Because my spelling is Wobbly. It's good spelling but it Wobbles, and the letters get in the wrong places. Would *you* write 'A Happy Birthday' on it for me?"

"It's a nice pot," said Owl, looking at it all round. "Couldn't I give it too? From both of us?"

"No," said Pooh. "That would *not* be a good plan. Now I'll just wash it first, and then you can write on it."

Well, he washed the pot out, and dried it, while Owl licked the end of his pencil, and wondered how to spell "birthday."

"Can you read, Pooh?" he asked, a little anxiously. "There's a notice about knocking and ringing outside my door, which Christopher Robin wrote. Could you read it?"

"Christopher Robin told me what it said, and *then* I could."

"Well, I'll tell you what this says, and then you'll be able to."

So Owl wrote . . . and this is what he wrote:

HIPY PAPY BTHUTHDTH THUTHDA
BTHUTHDY.

Pooh looked on admiringly.

"I'm just saying 'A Happy Birthday,' " said Owl carelessly.

"It's a nice long one," said Pooh, very much impressed by it.

"Well, *actually,* of course, I'm saying 'A Very Happy Birthday with love from Pooh.' Naturally it takes a good deal of pencil to say a long thing like that."

"Oh, I see," said Pooh.

Gallant Piglet (PIGLET)! Ho!

In which Piglet is revealed as intelligent, sensitive, and pluckish (but has a little problem with Heffalumps).

To start at the beginning: Piglet was one of the original toys of Christopher Milne. "Piglet was a present from a neighbour who lived over the way, a present for the small boy she so often used to meet out walking with his nanny."

From *Winnie-the-Pooh*, "Introduction":

. . . Piglet comes in for a good many things which Pooh misses; because you can't take Pooh to school without everybody knowing it, but Piglet is so small that he slips into a pocket, where it is very comfortable to feel him when you are not quite sure whether twice seven is twelve or twenty-two. Sometimes he slips out and has a good look in the ink-pot, and in this way he has got more education than Pooh, but 67

Pooh doesn't mind. Some have brains, and some haven't, he says, and there it is.

From *Winnie-the-Pooh:*

The Piglet lived in a very grand house in the middle of a beech-tree, and the beech-tree was in the middle of the forest, and the Piglet lived in the middle of the house. Next to his house was a piece of broken board which had: "TRESPASSERS W" on it. When Christopher Robin asked the Piglet what it meant, he said it was his grandfather's name, and had been in the family for a long time. Christopher

Robin said you *couldn't* be called Trespassers
W, and Piglet said yes, you could,
because his grandfather was, and it
was short for Trespassers Will,
which was short for Trespassers
William. And his grandfather had
had two names in case he lost one—Trespassers after an
uncle, and William after Trespassers.

"I've got two names," said Christopher Robin carelessly.

"Well, there you are, that proves it," said Piglet.

Piglet appears in almost every Pooh story (and of all the Animals, he is the one to whom Pooh turns so often when out adventuring or waiting for Hums to come to him), and of all the Animals he is the one who changes the most through the two books. Piglet shows MORE Pluck, reveals MORE Brains (or Fluff, if you must), and appears MORE Piglet.

There are many fine things about Piglet. Eeyore of all people appreciates Piglet for being, well, so Piglet. The case can be put as follows (that is, if a case need be made): Eeyore's Concern for Piglet's Well-being, as when he was told Piglet had fallen down while bringing him a birthday present, " 'Dear, dear, how unlucky! You ran too fast, I expect. You didn't hurt yourself, Little Piglet?' " And then there is Eeyore's Appreciation of Piglet's Size, " 'About as big as Piglet,' Eeyore said to himself sadly. 'My favourite size. Well, well.' " And then again, there is Eeyore's Appreciation of Piglet's Company, " 'Christopher Robin and I are going for a Short Walk,' he said, 'not a Jostle. If he likes to bring Pooh and Piglet with him, I shall be glad of their company . . .' "

(And Piglet too shows concern for Eeyore.)

From *The House At Pooh Corner:*

Piglet got up early that morning to pick himself a bunch of violets; and when he had picked them and put them in a pot in the middle of his house, it suddenly came over him that nobody had ever picked Eeyore a bunch of violets, and the more he thought of this, the more he thought how sad it was to be an Animal who had never had a bunch of violets picked for him. So he hurried out again, saying to himself, "Eeyore, Violets," and then "Violets, Eeyore," in case he forgot, because it was that sort of day, and he picked a large bunch and trotted along, smelling them, and feeling very happy . . .

Piglet is a very considerate animal. He not only helps build Eeyore a new and better home, he even gives his own home to Owl when Owl becomes, well, without his after a Very Very Blusterous Day. Piglet never hesitates when Christopher Robin calls for an Expotition and Rabbit organizes a Search for Small. . . . That is, Piglet does hesitate just a little, as a Very Small Animal must, but that doesn't stop him from doing things. It is hard when you don't have much Size, but in the end, having faced up to Heffalumps, Woozles, Wizzles, a Fiercer Animal Deprived of Its Young, Jagulars, and other assorted Fierce Animals, Piglet shows Great Pluck facing up to Flooding, Blusterous Days, Falling Houses, and having to Climb out of Owl's letter-box.

From *Winnie-the-Pooh*:

By and by Piglet woke up. As soon as he woke he said to himself, "Oh!" Then he said bravely, "Yes," and then, still more bravely, "Quite so." But he didn't feel very brave, for the word which was really jiggeting about in his brain was "Heffalumps."

What was a Heffalump like?

Was it Fierce?

Did it come when you whistled? And *how* did it come?

Was it Fond of Pigs at all?

If it was Fond of Pigs, did it make any difference *what sort of Pig?*

Supposing it was Fierce with Pigs, would it make any difference *if the Pig had a grandfather called TRESPASSERS WILLIAM?*

(And Piglet shows more Brains than the Others give him credit for. He knows what to do when meeting Heffalumps.)

From *The House At Pooh Corner:*

"Pooh!" cried Piglet, and now it was *his* turn to be the admiring one. "You've saved us!"

"Have I?" said Pooh, not feeling quite sure.

But Piglet was quite sure; and his mind ran on, and he saw Pooh and the Heffalump talking to each other, and he thought suddenly, and a little sadly, that it *would* have been rather nice if it had been Piglet and the Heffalump talking so grandly to each other, and not Pooh, much as he loved Pooh; because he really had more brain than Pooh, and the conversation would go better if he and not Pooh were doing one side of it, and it would be comforting afterwards in the evenings to look back on the day when he answered a Heffalump back as bravely as if the Heffalump wasn't there. It seemed so easy now. He knew just what he would say:

HEFFALUMP *(gloatingly):* "Ho-*ho!*"

PIGLET *(carelessly):* "Tra-la-la, tra-la-la."

HEFFALUMP *(surprised, and not quite so sure of himself):* "Ho-*ho!*"

PIGLET *(more carelessly still):* "Tiddle-um-tum, tiddle-um-tum."

HEFFALUMP *(beginning to say Ho-ho and turning it awkwardly into a cough):* "H'r'm! What's all this?"

PIGLET *(surprised):* "Hullo! This is a trap I've made, and I'm waiting for a Heffalump to fall into it."

HEFFALUMP *(greatly disappointed):* "Oh!" *(after a long silence):* "Are you sure?"

PIGLET: "Yes."

HEFFALUMP: "Oh!" *(nervously):* "I—I thought it was a trap *I'd* made to catch Piglets."

PIGLET *(surprised):* "Oh, no!"

HEFFALUMP: "Oh!" *(apologetically):* "I—I must have got it wrong, then."

PIGLET: "I'm afraid so." *(politely):* "I'm sorry." *(He goes on humming.)*

HEFFALUMP: "Well—well—I—well. I suppose I'd better be getting back?"

PIGLET *(looking up carelessly):* "Must you? Well, if you see Christopher Robin anywhere, you might tell him I want him."

HEFFALUMP *(eager to please):* "Certainly! Certainly!" *(He hurries off.)*

POOH *(who wasn't going to be there, but we find we can't do without him):* "Oh, Piglet, how brave and clever you are!"

PIGLET *(modestly):* "Not at all, Pooh." *(And then, when Christopher Robin comes, Pooh can tell him all about it.)*

Finally, Piglet, to the admiration (and relief) of his friends, does something of Great Bravery—an act that deserves its own Respectful Pooh Song. From the first time we meet Piglet until the moment we leave him, Piglet has done so much as a Very Small Animal.

From *The House At Pooh Corner:*

Pooh followed slowly. He had something better to do than to find a new house for Owl; he had to make up a Pooh song about the old one. Because he had promised Piglet days and days ago that he would, and whenever he and Piglet had met since, Piglet didn't actually say anything, but you knew at once why he didn't; and if anybody mentioned Hums or Trees or String or Storms-in-the-Night, Piglet's nose went all pink at the tip and he talked about something quite different in a hurried sort of way.

"But it isn't Easy," said Pooh to himself, as he looked at what had once been Owl's House. "Because Poetry and Hums aren't things which you get, they're things which get you. And all you can do is to go where they can find you."

He waited hopefully. . . .

"Well," said Pooh after a long wait, "I shall begin 'Here lies a tree' because it does, and then I'll see what happens."

This is what happened.

> *Here lies a tree which Owl (a bird)*
> *Was fond of when it stood on end,*
> *And Owl was talking to a friend*
> *Called Me (in case you hadn't heard)*
> *When something Oo occurred.*

> *For lo! the wind was blusterous*
> *And flattened out his favourite tree;*
> *And things looks bad for him and we—*
> *Looked bad, I mean, for he and us—*
> *I've never known them wuss.*

> *Then Piglet (PIGLET) thought a thing:*
> *"Courage!" he said. "There's always hope.*
> *I want a thinnish piece of rope.*

Or, if there isn't any bring
A thickish piece of string."

So to the letter-box he rose,
  While Pooh and Owl said "Oh!"
    and "Hum!"
  And where the letters always come
(Called "LETTERS ONLY") Piglet sqoze
His head and then his toes.

O gallant Piglet (PIGLET)! Ho!
  Did Piglet tremble? Did he blinch?
  No, No, he struggled inch by inch
Through LETTERS ONLY, as I know
Because I saw him go.

He ran and ran, and then he stood
  And shouted, "Help for Owl, a bird
  And Pooh, a bear!" until he heard
The others coming through the wood
As quickly as they could.

"Help-help and Rescue!" Piglet cried
  And showed the others where to go.
  Sing ho! for Piglet (PIGLET) ho!
And soon the door was opened wide
And we were both outside!

Sing ho! for Piglet, ho!
Ho!

From *The House At Pooh Corner:*

"There!" said Eeyore proudly, stopping them outside Piglet's house. "And the name on it, and everything!"

"Oh!" cried Christopher Robin, wondering whether to laugh or what.

"Just the house for Owl. Don't you think so, little Piglet?"

And then Piglet did a Noble Thing, and he did it in a sort of dream, while he was thinking of all the wonderful words Pooh had hummed about him.

"Yes, it's just the house for Owl," he said grandly. "And I hope he'll be very happy in it." And then he gulped twice, because he had been very happy in it himself.

"What do *you* think, Christopher Robin?" asked Eeyore a little anxiously, feeling that something wasn't quite right.

Christopher Robin had a question to ask first, and he was wondering how to ask it.

"Well," he said at last, "it's a very nice house, and if your own house is blown down, you *must* go somewhere else, mustn't you, Piglet? What would *you* do, if *your* house was blown down?"

Before Piglet could think, Pooh answered for him.

"He'd come and live with me," said Pooh, "wouldn't you, Piglet?"

Piglet squeezed his paw.

"Thank you, Pooh," he said, "I should love to."

> *Sing ho! for Piglet, ho!*
> *Ho!*
> *O gallant Piglet (PIGLET)! Ho!*

Gloomy Animal: Eeyore the Old Grey Donkey

In which we are given some insightful deliberations about life and the weather by an old grey donkey, and we are told about the importance of Exchanging Thought.

Of all the Animals in the Forest, only two (that is, 2) have proper names. Now, Owl is an owl, Rabbit is a rabbit, Tigger is a tigger, Kanga is a kanga with Roo as a roo (although more properly, he is a Joey.*) But you see what I mean. Bear is called Edward or Pooh or Winnie-ther-Pooh. And Donkey is called Eeyore. More significantly, Bear and Donkey not only have proper names; their full names make them special: not just Winnie but Winnie-ther-Pooh, and not just Eeyore but Eeyore the Old Grey Donkey.*

You see? Eeyore has depth, has Eeyore. Not just "Donkey"— Eeyore is somebody.

And he is somebody almost always misunderstood. . . .

From *The Nation,* November 21, 1928:

THE HOUSE AT POOH CORNER.
By A. A. Milne. E. P. Dutton and Company. $2.50.

Since this volume ten days after publication was in its fifty-first edition there seems to be nothing one can say for or against it which will be of the slightest use or interest to anybody. "The House at Pooh Corner" might be called the "Abie's Irish Rose" of juvenile literature if it were not for the fact that, with all its unrestrained whimsy, it is a nice little book. The gloomy and sardonic Eeyore is by far the most attractive character in it.

Eeyore may appear gloomy, and he may seem sardonic, but for all that, he is highly likable (and he was a favorite of Mr. Shepard, who said, "I have such sympathy for Eeyore always").

In origins, as Christopher Milne informs us, "Eeyore, too, was an early present. Perhaps in his younger days he had held his head higher, but by the time the stories came to be written his neck had gone like that and this had given him his gloomy disposition."

Perhaps Eeyore only appears *more gloomy than he actually is. Even if a case cannot be made that Eeyore the Old Grey Donkey gallops round the thistly bits of the Forest like a young whatever-young-donkeys-are-called,* he *shows himself to be a kind, thoughtful Animal.*

And not like some.

All in all, Eeyore thinks, *he* ponders, *he uses* Brains.

From *Winnie-the-Pooh:*

The Old Grey Donkey, Eeyore, stood by himself in a thistly corner of the forest, his front feet well apart, his head on one side, and thought about things. Sometimes he thought sadly to himself, "Why?" and sometimes he thought, "Wherefore?" and sometimes he thought, "Inasmuch as which?"—and some- times he didn't quite know what he was thinking about. So when Winnie-the-Pooh came stumping along, Eeyore was very glad to be able to stop thinking for a little, in order to say "How do you do?" in a gloomy manner to him.

"And how are you?" said Winnie-the-Pooh.

Eeyore shook his head from side to side.

"Not very how," he said. "I don't seem to have felt at all how for a long time."

From *The House At Pooh Corner:*

"Hallo, Eeyore," said Christopher Robin, as he opened the door and came out. "How are *you?*"

"It's snowing still," said Eeyore gloomily.

"So it is."

"*And* freezing."

"Is it?"

"Yes," said Eeyore. "However," he said, brightening up a little, "we haven't had an earthquake lately."

Eeyore has his interests—his hobbies, *if one can say this of a donkey and not a horse—which include* meteorol*—whatever that thing is to do with the weather.*

From *The House At Pooh Corner:*

"I don't know how it is, Christopher Robin, but what with all this snow and one thing and another, not to men-

tion icicles and such-like, it isn't so Hot in my field about three o'clock in the morning as some people think it is. It isn't Close, if you know what I mean—not so as to be uncomfortable. It isn't Stuffy. In fact, Christopher Robin," he went on in a loud whisper, "quite-be-tween-ourselves-and-don't-tell-anybody, it's Cold."

From *The House At Pooh Corner:*

"I shouldn't be surprised if it hailed a good deal tomorrow," Eeyore was saying. "Blizzards and what-not. Being fine today doesn't

Mean Anything. It has no sig—what's that word? Well, it has none of that. It's just a small piece of weather."

Eeyore's generosity is boundless. Even if the habits of Bouncing Animals such as Tiggers are somewhat distressing, Eeyore still shows himself to have a generous nature, especially when it comes to sharing his favorite patch of thistles.

From *The House At Pooh Corner:*

Eeyore walked all round Tigger one way, and then turned and walked all round him the other way.

"What did you say it was?" he asked.

"Tigger."

"Ah!" said Eeyore.

"He's just come," explained Piglet.

"Ah!" said Eeyore again.

He thought for a long time and then said:

"When is he going?"

Pooh explained to Eeyore that Tigger was a great friend of Christopher Robin's, who had come to stay in the Forest, and Piglet explained to Tigger that he mustn't mind what Eeyore said because he was *always* gloomy; and Eeyore explained to Piglet that, on the contrary, he was feeling particularly cheerful this morning; and Tigger explained to anybody who was listening that he hadn't had any breakfast yet.

"I knew there was something," said Pooh. "Tiggers always eat thistles, so that was why we came to see you, Eeyore."

"Don't mention it, Pooh."

"Oh, Eeyore, I didn't mean that I didn't *want* to see you—"

"Quite—quite. But your new stripy friend—naturally, he wants his breakfast. What did you say his name was?"

"Tigger."

"Then come this way, Tigger."

Eeyore led the way to the most thistly-looking patch of thistles that ever was, and waved a hoof at it.

"A little patch I was keeping for my birthday," he said; "but, after all, what are birthdays? Here today and gone to-morrow. Help yourself, Tigger."

Tigger thanked him and looked a little anxiously at Pooh.

"Are these really thistles?" he whispered.

"Yes," said Pooh.

"What Tiggers like best?"

"That's right," said Pooh.

"I see," said Tigger.

So he took a large mouthful, and he gave a large crunch.

"*Ow!*" said Tigger.

He sat down and put his paw in his mouth.

"What's the matter?" asked Pooh.

"*Hot!*" mumbled Tigger.

"Your friend," said Eeyore, "appears to have bitten on a bee."

Pooh's friend stopped shaking his head to get the prickles out, and explained that Tiggers didn't like thistles.

"Then why bend a perfectly good one?" asked Eeyore.

Eeyore is a connoisseur of thistles (that is, he knows his thistles), and because he is also a philosophizing type of Animal, he is not above philosophizing over food—that is, talking about the right way to eat as well as the better way to eat. Or something.

From *Winnie-the-Pooh:*

"I think," said Christopher Robin, "that we ought to eat all our Provisions now, so that we shan't have so much to carry."

"Eat all our what?" said Pooh.

"All that we've brought," said Piglet, getting to work.

"That's a good idea," said Pooh, and he got to work too.

"Have you all got something?" asked Christopher Robin with his mouth full.

"All except me," said Eeyore. "As Usual." He looked round at them in his melancholy way. "I suppose none of you are sitting on a thistle by any chance?"

"I believe I am," said Pooh. "Ow!" He got up, and looked behind him. "Yes, I was. I thought so."

"Thank you, Pooh. If you've quite finished with it." He moved across to Pooh's place, and began to eat.

"It don't do them any Good, you know, sitting on them," he went on, as he looked up munching. "Takes all the Life out of them. Remember that another time, all of you. A little Consideration, a little Thought for Others, makes all the difference."

Finally—that is, to end this all off—the affectionate nature of Eyore, or, more properly put, his sensitive nature, is seen when we read about the loss of his tail.

From *Winnie-the-Pooh:*

"Dear, dear," said Pooh, "I'm sorry about that. Let's have a look at you."

So Eeyore stood there, gazing sadly at the ground, and Winnie-the-Pooh walked all round him once.

"Why, what's happened to your tail?" he said in surprise.

"What *has* happened to it?" said Eeyore.

"It isn't there!"

"Are you sure?"

"Well, either a tail *is* or it isn't there. You can't make a mistake about it. And yours *isn't* there!"

"Then what is?"

"Nothing."

"Let's have a look," said Eeyore, and he turned slowly round to the place where his tail had been a little while ago, and then, finding that he couldn't catch it up, he turned round the other way, until he came back to where he was at first, and then he put his head down and looked between his front legs, and at last he said, with a long, sad sigh, "I believe you're right."

"Of course I'm right," said Pooh.

"That Accounts for a Good Deal," said Eeyore gloomily. "It Explains Everything. No Wonder."

From *Winnie-the-Pooh:*

"Handsome bell-rope, isn't it?" said Owl.

Pooh nodded.

"It reminds me of something," he said, "but I can't think what. Where did you get it?"

"I just came across it in the Forest. It was hanging over a bush, and I thought at first somebody lived there, so I rang it, and nothing happened, and then I rang it again very loudly, and it came off in my hand, and as nobody seemed to want it, I took it home, and—"

"Owl," said Pooh solemnly, "you made a mistake. Somebody did want it."

"Who?"

"Eeyore. My dear friend Eeyore. He was—he was fond of it."

"Fond of it?"

"Attached to it," said Winnie-the-Pooh sadly.

From *Winnie-the-Pooh:*

"Thank you, Christopher Robin. You're the only one who seems to understand about tails. They don't think—that's what's the matter with some of these others. They've no imagination. A tail isn't a tail to them, it's just a Little Bit Extra at the back."

"Never mind, Eeyore," said Christopher Robin, rubbing his hardest. "Is *that* better?"

"It's feeling more like a tail perhaps. It Belongs again, if you know what I mean."

Eeyore may not be part of the Social Round in the Forest, but friendship, fellowship, and the proper Exchange of Thought are very important to him. . . .

From *Winnie-the-Pooh:*

"I might have known," said Eeyore. "After all, one can't complain. I have my friends. Somebody spoke to me only yesterday. And it was last week or the week before that Rabbit bumped into me and said 'Bother!' The Social Round. Always something going on."

Nobody was listening. . . .

From *The House At Pooh Corner:*

"Hallo, Eeyore," they called out cheerfully.

"Ah!" said Eeyore. "Lost your way?"

"We just came to see you," said Piglet. "And to see how your house was. Look, Pooh, it's still standing!"

"I know," said Eeyore. "Very odd. Somebody ought to have come down and pushed it over."

"We wondered whether the wind would blow it down," said Pooh.

"Ah, that's why nobody's bothered, I suppose. I thought perhaps they'd forgotten."

"Well, we're very glad to see you, Eeyore, and now we're going to see Owl."

"That's right. You'll like Owl. He flew past a day or two ago and noticed me. He didn't actually say anything, mind you, but he knew it was me. Very friendly of him, I thought. Encouraging."

Pooh and Piglet shuffled about a little and said, "Well, good-bye, Eeyore" as lingeringly as they could, but they had a long way to go, and wanted to be getting on.

"Good-bye," said Eeyore. "Mind you don't get blown away, little Piglet. You'd be missed. People would say 'Where's little Piglet been blown to?'—really wanting to know. Well, good-bye. And thank you for happening to pass me."

From *The House At Pooh Corner:*

"What's the matter with his old house?" asked Eeyore. Rabbit explained.

"Nobody tells me," said Eeyore. "Nobody keeps me Informed. I make it seventeen days come Friday since anybody spoke to me."

"It certainly isn't seventeen days—"

"Come Friday," explained Eeyore.

"And today's Saturday," said Rabbit. "So that would make it eleven days. And I was here myself a week ago."

"Not conversing," said Eeyore. "Not first one and then the other. You said 'Hallo' and Flashed Past. I saw your tail in the distance as I was meditating my reply. I *had* thought of saying 'What?'—but, of course, it was then too late."

"Well, I was in a hurry."

"No Give and Take," Eeyore went on. "No Exchange of Thought: *'Hallo—What'*—I mean, it gets you nowhere, particularly if the other person's tail is only just in sight for the second half of the conversation."

"It's your fault, Eeyore. You've never been to see any of us. You just stay here in this one corner of the Forest waiting for the others to come to *you*. Why don't you go to *them* sometimes?"

Eeyore was silent for a little while, thinking.

"There may be something in what you say, Rabbit," he said at last. "I must move about more. I must come and go."

"That's right, Eeyore. Drop in on any of us at any time, when you feel like it."

"Thank-you, Rabbit. And if anybody says in a Loud Voice 'Bother, it's Eeyore,' I can drop out again."

Rabbit stood on one leg for a moment.

"Well," he said, "I must be going."

"Good-bye," said Eeyore.

From *The House At Pooh Corner:*

POOH INVENTS A NEW GAME AND EEYORE JOINS IN

. . . Now one day Pooh and Piglet and Rabbit and Roo were all playing Poohsticks together. They had dropped their sticks in when Rabbit said "Go!" and then they had hurried across to the other side of the bridge, and now they were all leaning over the edge, waiting to see whose stick would come out first. But it was a long time coming, because the river was very lazy that day, and hardly seemed to mind if it didn't ever get there at all.

"I can see mine!" cried Roo. "No, I can't, it's something else. Can you see yours, Piglet? I thought I could see mine, but I couldn't. There it is! No, it isn't. Can you see yours, Pooh?"

"No," said Pooh.

"I expect my stick's stuck," said Roo. "Rabbit, my stick's stuck. Is your stick stuck, Piglet?"

"They always take longer than you think," said Rabbit.

"How long do you *think* they'll take?" asked Roo.

"I can see yours, Piglet," said Pooh suddenly.

"Mine's a sort of greyish one," said Piglet, not daring to lean too far over in case he fell in.

"Yes, that's what I can see. It's coming over on to my side."

Rabbit leant over further than ever, looking for his, and Roo wriggled up and down, calling out "Come on, stick! Stick, stick, stick!" and Piglet got very excited because his was the only one which had been seen, and that meant that he was winning.

"It's coming!" said Pooh.

"Are you *sure* it's mine?" squeaked Piglet excitedly.

"Yes, because it's grey. A big grey one. Here it comes! A very—big—grey—Oh, no, it isn't, it's Eeyore."

And out floated Eeyore.

"Eeyore!" cried everybody.

Looking very calm, very dignified, with his legs in the air, came Eeyore from beneath the bridge.

"It's Eeyore!" cried Roo, terribly excited.

"Is that so?" said Eeyore, getting caught up by a little eddy, and turning slowly round three times. "I wondered."

"I didn't know you were playing," said Roo.

"I'm not," said Eeyore.

"Eeyore, what *are* you doing there?" said Rabbit.

"I'll give you three guesses, Rabbit. Digging holes in the ground? Wrong. Leaping from branch to branch of a young oak-tree? Wrong. Waiting for somebody to help me out of the river? Right. Give Rabbit time, and he'll always get the answer."

"But, Eeyore," said Pooh in distress, "what can we—I mean, how shall we—do you think if we—"

"Yes," said Eeyore. "One of those would be just the thing. Thank you, Pooh."

"He's going *round* and *round,*" said Roo, much impressed.

"And why not?" said Eeyore coldly.

"I can swim too," said Roo proudly.

"Not round and round," said Eeyore. "It's much more difficult. I didn't want to come swimming at all today," he went on, revolving slowly. "But if, when in, I decide to practise a slight circular movement from right to left—or perhaps I should say," he added, as he got into another eddy, "from left to right, just as it happens to occur to me, it is nobody's business but my own."

There was a moment's silence while everybody thought.

"I've got a sort of idea," said Pooh at last, "but I don't suppose it's a very good one."

"I don't suppose it is either," said Eeyore.

"Go on, Pooh," said Rabbit. "Let's have it."

"Well, if we all threw stones and things into the river on *one* side of Eeyore, the stones would make waves, and the waves would wash him to the other side."

"That's a very good idea," said Rabbit, and Pooh looked happy again.

"Very," said Eeyore. "When I want to be washed, Pooh, I'll let you know."

"Supposing we hit him by mistake?" said Piglet anxiously.

"Or supposing you missed him by mistake," said Eeyore. "Think of all the possibilities, Piglet, before you settle down to enjoy yourselves."

But Pooh had got the biggest stone he could carry, and was leaning over the bridge, holding it in his paws.

"I'm not throwing it, I'm dropping it, Eeyore," he explained. "And then I can't miss—I mean I can't hit you. *Could* you stop turning round for a moment, because it muddles me rather?"

"No," said Eeyore. "I *like* turning round."

Rabbit began to feel that it was time he took command.

"Now, Pooh," he said, "when I say 'Now!' you can drop it. Eeyore, when I say 'Now!' Pooh will drop his stone."

"Thank you very much, Rabbit, but I expect I shall know."

"Are you ready, Pooh? Piglet, give Pooh a little more room. Get back a bit there, Roo. Are you ready?"

"No," said Eeyore.

"Now!" said Rabbit.

Pooh dropped his stone. There was a loud splash, and Eeyore disappeared. . . .

It was an anxious moment for the watchers on the bridge. They looked and looked . . . and even the sight of Piglet's stick coming out a little in front of Rabbit's didn't cheer them up as much as you would have expected. And then, just as Pooh was beginning to think that he must have chosen the wrong stone or the wrong river or the wrong day for his Idea, something grey showed for a moment by the river bank . . . and it got slowly bigger and bigger . . . and at last it was Eeyore coming out.

With a shout they rushed off the bridge, and pushed and pulled at him; and soon he was standing among them again on dry land.

"Oh, Eeyore, you *are* wet!" said Piglet, feeling him.

Eeyore shook himself, and asked somebody to explain to Piglet what happened when you had been inside a river for quite a long time.

"Well done, Pooh," said Rabbit kindly. "That was a good idea of ours."

"What was?" asked Eeyore.

"Hooshing you to the bank like that."

"*Hooshing* me?" said Eeyore in surprise. "Hooshing *me?* You didn't think I was *hooshed,* did you? I dived. Pooh dropped a large stone on me, and so as not to be struck heavily on the chest, I dived and swam to the bank."

"You didn't really," whispered Piglet to Pooh, so as to comfort him.

"I didn't *think* I did," said Pooh anxiously.

"It's just Eeyore," said Piglet. "*I* thought your Idea was a very good Idea."

Pooh began to feel a little more comfortable, because when you are a Bear of Very Little Brain, and you Think of Things, you find sometimes that a Thing which seemed very Thingish inside you is quite different when it gets out into the open and has other people looking at it. And, anyhow, Eeyore *was* in the river, and now he *wasn't,* so he hadn't done any harm.

"How did you fall in, Eeyore?" asked Rabbit, as he dried him with Piglet's handkerchief.

"I didn't," said Eeyore.

"But how—"

"I was BOUNCED," said Eeyore.

"Oo," said Roo excitedly, "did somebody push you?"

"Somebody BOUNCED me. I was just thinking by the side of the river—thinking, if any of you know what that means, when I received a loud BOUNCE."

"Oh, Eeyore!" said everybody.

"Are you sure you didn't slip?" asked Rabbit wisely.

"Of course I slipped. If you're standing on the slippery

bank of a river, and somebody BOUNCES you loudly from behind, you slip. What did you think I did?"

"But who did it?" asked Roo.

Eeyore didn't answer.

"I expect it was Tigger," said Piglet nervously.

"But, Eeyore," said Pooh, "was it a Joke, or an Accident? I mean—"

"I didn't stop to ask, Pooh. Even at the very bottom of the river I didn't stop to say to myself, '*Is* this a Hearty Joke, or is it the Merest Accident?' I just floated to the surface, and said to myself, 'It's wet.' If you know what I mean."

"And where was Tigger?" asked Rabbit.

Before Eeyore could answer, there was a loud noise behind them, and through the hedge came Tigger himself.

"Hallo, everybody," said Tigger cheerfully.

"Hallo, Tigger," said Roo.

Rabbit became very important suddenly.

"Tigger," he said solemnly, "what happened just now?"

"Just when?" said Tigger a little uncomfortably.

"When you bounced Eeyore into the river."

"I didn't bounce him."

"You bounced me," said Eeyore gruffly.

"I didn't really. I had a cough, and I happened to be behind Eeyore, and I said '*Grrrr—oppp—ptschschschz.*'"

"Why?" said Rabbit, helping Piglet up, and dusting him. "It's all right, Piglet."

"It took me by surprise," said Piglet nervously.

"That's what I call bouncing," said Eeyore. "Taking people by surprise. Very unpleasant habit. I don't mind Tigger being in the Forest," he went on, "because it's a large Forest, and there's plenty of room to bounce in it. But I don't see why he should come into *my* little corner of it, and bounce there. It isn't as if there was anything very wonderful about my little corner. Of course for people who like cold, wet, ugly bits it *is* something rather special, but otherwise it's just a corner, and if anybody feels bouncy—"

"I didn't bounce, I coughed," said Tigger crossly.

"Bouncy or coffy, it's all the same at the bottom of the river."

"Well," said Rabbit, "all I can say is—well, here's Christopher Robin, so *he* can say it."

Christopher Robin came down from the Forest to the bridge, feeling all sunny and careless, and just as if twice nineteen didn't matter a bit, as it didn't on such a happy afternoon, and he thought that if he stood on the bottom rail of the bridge, and leant over, and watched the river slipping slowly away beneath him, then he would suddenly know everything that there was to be known, and he would be able to tell Pooh, who wasn't quite sure about some of it. But when he got to the bridge and saw all the animals there, then he knew that it wasn't that kind of afternoon, but the other kind, when you wanted to *do* something.

"It's like this, Christopher Robin," began Rabbit. "Tigger—"

"No, I didn't," said Tigger.

"Well, anyhow, there I was," said Eeyore.

"But I don't think he meant to," said Pooh.

"He just *is* bouncy," said Piglet, "and he can't help it."

"Try bouncing *me*, Tigger," said Roo eagerly. "Eeyore, Tigger's going to try *me*. Piglet, do you think—"

"Yes, yes," said Rabbit, "we don't all want to speak at once. The point is, what does Christopher Robin think about it?"

"All I did was I coughed," said Tigger.

"He bounced," said Eeyore.

"Well, I sort of boffed," said Tigger.

"Hush!" said Rabbit, holding up his paw. "What does Christopher Robin think about it all? That's the point."

"Well," said Christopher Robin, not quite sure what it was all about, "*I* think—"

"Yes?" said everybody.

"*I* think we all ought to play Poohsticks."

So they did. And Eeyore, who had never played it before, won more times than anybody else; and Roo fell in twice, the first time by accident and the second time on purpose, because he suddenly saw Kanga coming from the Forest, and he knew he'd have to go to bed anyhow. So then Rabbit said he'd go with them; and Tigger and Eeyore went off together, because Eeyore wanted to tell Tigger How to Win at Poohsticks, which you do by letting your stick drop in a twitchy sort of way, if you understand what I mean, Tigger; and Christopher Robin and Pooh and Piglet were left on the bridge by themselves.

For a long time they looked at the river beneath them, saying nothing, and the river said nothing too, for it felt very quiet and peaceful on this summer afternoon.

"Tigger is all right *really*," said Piglet lazily.

"Of course he is," said Christopher Robin.

"Everybody is *really,*" said Pooh. "That's what *I* think," said Pooh. "But I don't suppose I'm right," he said.

"Of course you are," said Christopher Robin.

Jumping Animals: Kanga and Roo, and Tigger (Who Bounces)

In which we don't discover why Tigger comes to the Forest (but we learn that he attacks Tablecloths; eats everybody's favorite food; is far too Bouncy, especially for Eeyore; and turns out to be all right really); and we find out how Kanga and Roo came to the Forest and why everybody quite liked them in the end.

Kanga, Roo, and Tigger were all late arrivals to the Forest— newcomers *is probably a better expression—and for some reason they jumped and bounced about, ended up living in the one place, and seemed to live on a diet of Medicines and Sandwiches. Like Pooh, they were actual toys belonging to Christopher Milne, but (and we mean* but) "*both Kanga and Tigger were later arrivals, presents from my parents, carefully chosen not just for the delight they might give to their new owner, but also for their literary possibilities." And, to confuse matters, in Mr. Milne's original draft, Kanga was a he, not a she. Luckily, an editor picked the problem up and sorted it all out before the book was published.*

Tigger bounces into the Forest, and he bounces all through the Forest. Tigger is just that sort of Animal. He is not shy, not quiet, not indifferent, and never bored. He bounces.

From *The House At Pooh Corner:*

Winnie-the-Pooh woke up suddenly in the middle of the night and listened. Then he got out of bed, and lit his candle, and stumped across the room to see if anybody was trying to get into his honey-cupboard, and they weren't, so he stumped back again, blew out his candle, and got into bed. Then he heard the noise again.

"Is that you, Piglet?" he said.

But it wasn't.

"Come in, Christopher Robin," he said.

But Christopher Robin didn't.

"Tell me about it tomorrow, Eeyore," said Pooh sleepily.

But the noise went on.

"Worraworraworraworraworra," said Whatever-it-was, and Pooh found that he wasn't asleep after all. . . .

He got out of bed and opened his front door.

"Hallo!" said Pooh, in case there was anything outside.

"Hallo!" said Whatever-it-was.

"Oh!" said Pooh. "Hallo!"

"Hallo!"

"Oh, *there* you are!" said Pooh. "Hallo!"

"Hallo!" said the Strange Animal, wondering how long this was going on.

Pooh was just going to say "Hallo!" for the fourth time when he thought that he wouldn't, so he said: "Who is it?" instead.

"Me," said a voice.

"Oh!" said Pooh. "Well, come here."

So Whatever-it-was came here, and in the light of the candle he and Pooh looked at each other.

"I'm Pooh," said Pooh.

"I'm Tigger," said Tigger.

"Oh!" said Pooh, for he had never seen an animal like this before. "Does Christopher Robin know about you?"

"Of course he does," said Tigger.

"Well," said Pooh, "it's the middle of the night, which is a good time for going to sleep. And tomorrow morning we'll have some honey for breakfast. Do Tiggers like honey?"

"They like everything," said Tigger cheerfully.

"Then if they like going to sleep on the floor, I'll go back to bed," said Pooh, "and we'll do things in the morning. Good night." And he got back into bed and went fast asleep.

When he awoke in the morning, the first thing he saw was Tigger, sitting in front of the glass and looking at himself.

"Hallo!" said Pooh.

"Hallo!" said Tigger. "I've found somebody just like me. I thought I was the only one of them."

Pooh got out of bed, and began to explain what a looking-glass was, but just as he was getting to the interesting part, Tigger said:

"Excuse me a moment, but there's something climbing up your table," and with one loud *Worraworraworraworraworra* he jumped at the end of the tablecloth, pulled it to the ground, wrapped himself up in it three times, rolled to the other end of the room, and, after a terrible struggle, got his head into the daylight again, and said cheerfully: "Have I won?"

"That's my tablecloth," said Pooh, as he began to unwind Tigger.

"I wondered what it was," said Tigger.

"It goes on the table and you put things on it."

"Then why did it try to bite me when I wasn't looking?"

"I don't *think* it did," said Pooh.

"It tried," said Tigger, "but I was too quick for it."

Pooh put the cloth back on the table, and he put a large honey-pot on the cloth, and they sat down to breakfast. And as soon as they sat down, Tigger took a large mouthful of honey . . . and he looked up at the ceiling with his head on one side, and made explor-

ing noises with his tongue and considering noises, and what-
have-we-got-*here* noises . . . and then he said in a very decided
voice:

"Tiggers don't like honey."

From *The House At Pooh Corner:*

> *What shall we do about*
> *poor little Tigger?*
> *If he never eats nothing he'll*
> *never get bigger.*
> *He doesn't like honey and haycorns*
> *and thistles*
> *Because of the taste and because of*
> *the bristles.*
> *And all the good things which an*
> *animal likes*
> *Have the wrong sort of swallow or*
> *too many spikes.*
>
> · · ·
>
> *But whatever his weight in pounds,*
> *shillings, and ounces,*
> *He always seems bigger*
> *because of his bounces.*

Rabbit did not like Tigger and his tiggerish bouncing, so he
wanted to teach him a lesson. "Well, I've got an idea," said Rab-
bit. And so the plan was to take Tigger deep into the Forest and
get him lost, and then Tigger would be sorry. But what happens?
Rabbit gets lost, that's what happens. . . .

From *The House At Pooh Corner:*

... Tigger was tearing round the Forest making loud yapping noises for Rabbit. And at last a very Small and Sorry Rabbit heard him. And the Small and Sorry Rabbit rushed through the mist at the noise, and it suddenly turned into a Tigger; a Friendly Tigger, a Grand Tigger, a Large and Helpful Tigger, a Tigger who bounced, if he bounced at all, in just the beautiful way a Tigger ought to bounce.

"Oh, Tigger, I *am* glad to see you," cried Rabbit.

Tigger finds a home with Kanga and Roo. Tigger may be interested in everything, want to do everything, and want to bounce everywhere (or everyone), but Tigger also needs kindness, as Kanga (a mother foremost) quickly understands.

From *The House At Pooh Corner:*

"Oh, there you are, Tigger!" said Christopher Robin. "I knew you'd be somewhere."

"I've been finding things in the Forest," said Tigger importantly. "I've found a pooh and a piglet and an eeyore, but I can't find any breakfast."

Pooh and Piglet came up and hugged Christopher Robin, and explained what had been happening.

"Don't *you* know what Tiggers like?" asked Pooh.

"I expect if I thought very hard I should," said Christopher Robin, "but I *thought* Tigger knew."

"I do," said Tigger. "Everything there is in the world except honey and haycorns and—what were those hot things called?"

"Thistles."

"Yes, and those."

"Oh, well then, Kanga can give you some breakfast."

So they went into Kanga's house, and when Roo had said, "Hallo, Pooh" and "Hallo, Piglet" once, and "Hallo, Tigger" twice, because he had never said it before and it sounded funny, they told Kanga what they wanted, and Kanga said very kindly, "Well, look in my cupboard, Tigger dear, and see what you'd like." Because she knew at once that, however big Tigger seemed to be, he wanted as much kindness as Roo.

Kanga is a mother, something even Rabbit couldn't dispute (although he found it quite unsettling). Here then are the "ATTRIBUTES OF MOTHERHOOD" (as displayed by Kanga, Mother of Roo):

1. Wants to Count Things ("like Roo's vests, and how many pieces of soap there were left, and the two clean spots on Tigger's feeder");
2. Makes sure you have sandwiches ("watercress sandwiches for Roo, and a packet of extract-of-malt sandwiches for Tigger");
3. Tells you what to do (that is, "to have a nice long morning in the Forest not getting into mischief");

4. Gives baths (with lots of soap);
5. Knows how to play a Joke.

From *Winnie-the-Pooh:*

KANGA AND BABY ROO COME TO THE FOREST,
AND PIGLET HAS A BATH

Nobody seemed to know where they came from, but there they were in the Forest: Kanga and Baby Roo. When Pooh asked Christopher Robin, "How did they come here?" Christopher Robin said, "In the Usual Way, if you know what I mean, Pooh," and Pooh, who didn't, said "Oh!" Then he nodded his head twice and said, "In the Usual Way. Ah!" Then he went to call upon his friend Piglet to see what *he* thought about it. And at Piglet's house he found Rabbit. So they all talked about it together.

"What I don't like about it is this," said Rabbit. "Here are we—you, Pooh, and you, Piglet, and Me—and suddenly—"

"And Eeyore," said Pooh.

"And Eeyore—and then suddenly—"

"And Owl," said Pooh.

"And Owl—and then all of a sudden—"

"Oh, and Eeyore," said Pooh. "I was forgetting *him.*"

"Here—we—are," said Rabbit very slowly and carefully, "all—of—us, and then, suddenly, we wake up one morning and, what do we find? We find a Strange Animal among us. An animal of whom we have never even heard before! An animal who carries her family about with her in her pocket!

Suppose I carried *my* family about with me in *my* pocket, how many pockets should I want?"

"Sixteen," said Piglet.

"Seventeen, isn't it?" said Rabbit. "And one more for a handkerchief—that's eighteen. Eighteen pockets in one suit! I haven't time."

There was a long and thoughtful silence . . . and then Pooh, who had been frowning very hard for some minutes, said: "*I* make it fifteen."

"What?" said Rabbit.

"Fifteen."

"Fifteen what?"

"Your family."

"What about them?"

Pooh rubbed his nose and said that he thought Rabbit had been talking about his family.

"Did I?" said Rabbit carelessly.

"Yes, you said—"

"Never mind, Pooh," said Piglet impatiently.

"The question is, What are we to do about Kanga?"

"Oh, I see," said Pooh.

"The best way," said Rabbit, "would be this. The best way would be to steal Baby Roo and hide him, and then when Kanga says, 'Where's Baby Roo?' we say, '*Aha!*'"

"*Aha!*" said Pooh, practising. "*Aha! Aha!* . . . Of course," he went on, "we could say '*Aha!*' even if we hadn't stolen Baby Roo."

"Pooh," said Rabbit kindly, "you haven't any brain."

"I know," said Pooh humbly.

"We say '*Aha!*' so that Kanga knows that *we* know where Baby Roo is. '*Aha!*' means 'We'll tell you where Baby Roo is, if you promise to go away from the Forest and never come back.' Now don't talk while I think."

Pooh went into a corner and tried saying "Aha!" in that sort of voice. Sometimes it seemed to him that it did mean what Rabbit said, and sometimes it seemed to him that it didn't. "I suppose it's just practise," he thought. "I wonder if Kanga will have to practise too so as to understand it."

"There's just one thing," said Piglet, fidgeting a bit. "I was talking to Christopher Robin, and he said that a Kanga was Generally Regarded as One of the Fiercer Animals. I am not frightened of Fierce Animals in the ordinary way, but it is well known that, if One of the Fiercer Animals is Deprived of Its Young, it becomes as fierce as Two of the Fiercer Animals. In which case 'Aha!' is perhaps a *foolish* thing to say."

"Piglet," said Rabbit, taking out a pencil, and licking the end of it, "you haven't any pluck."

"It is hard to be brave," said Piglet, sniffing slightly, "when you're only a Very Small Animal."

Rabbit, who had begun to write very busily, looked up and said:

"It is because you are a very small animal that you will be Useful in the adventure before us."

Piglet was so excited at the idea of being Useful that he forgot to be frightened any more, and when Rabbit went on to say that Kangas were only Fierce during the winter months, being at other times of an Affectionate Disposition, he could hardly sit still, he was so eager to begin being useful at once.

"What about me?" said Pooh sadly. "I suppose *I* shan't be useful?"

"Never mind, Pooh," said Piglet comfortingly. "Another time perhaps."

"Without Pooh," said Rabbit solemnly as he sharpened his pencil, "the adventure would be impossible."

"Oh!" said Piglet, and tried not to look disappointed. But Pooh went into a corner of the room and said proudly to himself, "Impossible without Me! *That* sort of Bear."

"Now listen all of you," said Rabbit when he had finished writing, and Pooh and Piglet sat listening very eagerly with their mouths open. This was what Rabbit read out:

PLAN TO CAPTURE BABY ROO

1. *General Remarks*. Kanga runs faster than any of Us, even Me.
2. *More General Remarks*. Kanga never takes her eye off Baby Roo, except when he's safely buttoned up in her pocket.
3. *Therefore*. If we are to capture Baby Roo, we must get a Long Start, because Kanga runs faster than any of Us, even Me. (*See* 1.)
4. *A Thought*. If Roo had jumped out of Kanga's pocket and Piglet had jumped in, Kanga wouldn't know the difference, because Piglet is a Very Small Animal.
5. Like Roo.
6. But Kanga would have to be looking the other way first, so as not to see Piglet jumping in.

7. See 2.
8. *Another Thought*. But if Pooh was talking to her very excitedly, she *might* look the other way for a moment.
9. And then I could run away with Roo.
10. Quickly.
11. *And Kanga wouldn't discover the difference until Afterwards.*

Well, Rabbit read this out proudly, and for a little while after he had read it nobody said anything. And then Piglet, who had been opening and shutting his mouth without making any noise, managed to say very huskily:

"And—Afterwards?"

"How do you mean?"

"When Kanga *does* Discover the Difference?"

"Then we all say *'Aha!'* "

"All three of us?"

"Yes."

"Oh!"

"Why, what's the trouble, Piglet?"

"Nothing," said Piglet, "as long as *we all three* say it. As long as we all three say it," said Piglet, "I don't mind," he said, "but I shouldn't care to say *'Aha!'* by myself. It wouldn't sound *nearly* so well. By the way," he said, "you *are* quite sure about what you said about the winter months?"

"The winter months?"

"Yes, only being Fierce in the Winter Months."

"Oh, yes, yes, that's all right. Well, Pooh? You see what you have to do?"

"No," said Pooh Bear. "Not yet," he said. "What *do* I do?"

"Well, you just have to talk very hard to Kanga so as she doesn't notice anything."

"Oh! What about?"

"Anything you like."

"You mean like telling her a little bit of poetry or some-thing?"

"That's it," said Rabbit. "Splendid. Now come along."

So they all went out to look for Kanga.

Kanga and Roo were spending a quiet afternoon in a sandy part of the Forest. Baby Roo was practising very small jumps in the sand, and falling down mouse-holes and climb-ing out of them, and Kanga was fidgeting about and saying "Just one more jump, dear, and then we must go home." And at that moment who should come stumping up the hill but Pooh.

"Good afternoon, Kanga."

"Good afternoon, Pooh."

"Look at me jumping," squeaked Roo, and fell into an-other mouse-hole.

"Hallo, Roo, my little fellow!"

"We were just going home," said Kanga. "Good afternoon, Rabbit. Good afternoon, Piglet."

Rabbit and Piglet, who had now come up from the other side of the hill, said, "Good afternoon," and "Hallo, Roo," and Roo asked them to look at him jumping, so they stayed and looked.

And Kanga looked too. . . .

"Oh, Kanga," said Pooh, after Rabbit had winked at him twice, "I don't know if you are interested in Poetry at all?"

"Hardly at all," said Kanga.

"Oh!" said Pooh.

"Roo, dear, just one more jump and then we must go home."

There was a short silence while Roo fell down another mouse-hole.

"Go on," said Rabbit in a loud whisper behind his paw.

"Talking of Poetry," said Pooh, "I made up a little piece as I was coming along. It went like this. Er—now let me see—"

"Fancy!" said Kanga. "Now Roo, dear—"

"You'll like this piece of poetry," said Rabbit.

"You'll love it," said Piglet.

"You must listen very carefully," said Rabbit.

"So as not to miss any of it," said Piglet.

"Oh, yes," said Kanga, but she still looked at Baby Roo.

"*How* did it go, Pooh?" said Rabbit.

Pooh gave a little cough and began.

LINES WRITTEN BY A BEAR OF VERY LITTLE BRAIN

On Monday, when the sun is hot
I wonder to myself a lot:
"Now is it true, or is it not,
"That what is which and which is what?"

On Tuesday, when it hails and snows,
The feeling on me grows and grows
That hardly anybody knows
If those are these or these are those.

On Wednesday, when the sky is blue,
And I have nothing else to do,
I sometimes wonder if it's true
That who is what and what is who.

On Thursday, when it starts to freeze
And hoar-frost twinkles on the trees,
How very readily one sees
That these are whose—but whose are these?

On Friday—

"Yes, it is, isn't it?" said Kanga, not waiting to hear what happened on Friday. "Just one more jump, Roo, dear, and then we really *must* be going."

Rabbit gave Pooh a hurrying-up sort of nudge.

"Talking of Poetry," said Pooh quickly, "have you ever noticed that tree right over there?"

"Where?" said Kanga. "Now, Roo—"

"Right over there," said Pooh, pointing behind Kanga's back.

"No," said Kanga. "Now jump in, Roo, dear, and we'll go home."

"You ought to look at that tree right over there," said Rabbit. "Shall I lift you in, Roo?" And he picked up Roo in his paws.

"I can see a bird in it from here," said Pooh. "Or is it a fish?"

"You ought to see that bird from here," said Rabbit. "Unless it's a fish."

"It isn't a fish, it's a bird," said Piglet.

"So it is," said Rabbit.

"Is it a starling or a blackbird?" said Pooh.

"That's the whole question," said Rabbit. "Is it a blackbird or a starling?"

And then at last Kanga did turn her head to look. And the moment that her head was turned, Rabbit said in a loud voice "In you go, Roo!" and in jumped Piglet into Kanga's pocket, and off scampered Rabbit, with Roo in his paws, as fast as he could.

"Why, where's Rabbit?" said Kanga, turning round again. "Are you all right, Roo, dear?"

Piglet made a squeaky Roo-noise from the bottom of Kanga's pocket.

"Rabbit had to go away," said Pooh. "I think he thought of something he had to go and see about suddenly."

"And Piglet?"

"I think Piglet thought of something at the same time. Suddenly."

"Well, we must be getting home," said Kanga. "Good-bye, Pooh." And in three large jumps she was gone.

Pooh looked after her as she went.

"I wish I could jump like that," he thought. "Some can and some can't. That's how it is."

But there were moments when Piglet wished that Kanga couldn't. Often, when he had had a long walk home through the Forest, he had wished that he were a bird; but now he thought jerkily to himself at the bottom of Kanga's pocket, "If this is flying I shall never really take to it."

And as he went up in the air, he said, *"Ooooooo!"* and as he came down he said, *"Ow!"* And he was saying, *"Ooooooo-ow, Ooooooo-ow, Ooooooo-ow"* all the way to Kanga's house.

Of course as soon as Kanga unbuttoned her pocket, she saw what had happened. Just for a moment, she thought she was frightened, and then she knew she wasn't; for she felt quite sure that Christopher Robin would never let any harm happen to Roo. So she said to herself, "If they are having a joke with me, I will have a joke with them."

"Now then, Roo, dear," she said, as she took Piglet out of her pocket. "Bed-time."

"Aha!" said Piglet, as well as he could after his Terrifying Journey. But it wasn't a very good *"Aha!"* and Kanga didn't seem to understand what it meant.

"Bath first," said Kanga in a cheerful voice.

"Aha!" said Piglet again, looking round anxiously for the

others. But the others weren't there. Rabbit was playing with Baby Roo in his own house, and feeling more fond of him every minute, and Pooh, who had decided to be a Kanga, was still at the sandy place on the top of the Forest, practising jumps.

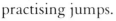

"I am not at all sure," said Kanga in a thoughtful voice, "that it wouldn't be a good idea to have a *cold* bath this evening. Would you like that, Roo, dear?"

Piglet, who had never been really fond of baths, shuddered a long indignant shudder, and said in as brave a voice as he could:

"Kanga, I see the time has come to spleak painly."

"Funny little Roo," said Kanga, as she got the bathwater ready.

"I am *not* Roo," said Piglet loudly. "I am Piglet!"

"Yes, dear, yes," said Kanga soothingly. "And imitating Piglet's voice too! So clever of him," she went on, as she took a large bar of yellow soap out of the cupboard. "What *will* he be doing next?"

"Can't you *see?*" shouted Piglet. "Haven't you got *eyes?* Look at me!"

"I *am* looking, Roo, dear," said Kanga rather severely. "And you know what I told you yesterday about making faces. If you go on making faces like Piglet's, you will grow

up to *look* like Piglet—and *then* think how sorry you will be. Now then, into the bath, and don't let me have to speak to you about it again."

Before he knew where he was, Piglet was in the bath, and Kanga was scrubbing him firmly with a large lathery flannel.

"Ow!" cried Piglet. "Let me out! I'm Piglet!"

"Don't open the mouth, dear, or the soap goes in," said Kanga. "There! What did I tell you?"

"You—you—you did it on purpose," spluttered Piglet, as soon as he could speak again . . . and then accidentally had another mouthful of lathery flannel.

"That's right, dear, don't say anything," said Kanga, and in another minute Piglet was out of the bath, and being rubbed dry with a towel.

"Now," said Kanga, "there's your medicine, and then bed."

"W-w-what medicine?" said Piglet.

"To make you grow big and strong, dear. You don't want to grow up small and weak like Piglet, do you? Well, then!"

At that moment there was a knock at the door.

"Come in," said Kanga, and in came Christopher Robin.

"Christopher Robin, Christopher Robin!" cried Piglet. "Tell Kanga who I am! She keeps saying I'm Roo. I'm *not* Roo, am I?"

Christopher Robin looked at him very carefully, and shook his head.

"You can't be Roo," he said, "because I've just seen Roo playing in Rabbit's house."

"Well!" said Kanga. "Fancy that! Fancy my making a mistake like that."

"There you are!" said Piglet. "I told you so. I'm Piglet."

Christopher Robin shook his head again.

"Oh, you're not Piglet," he said. "I know Piglet well, and he's *quite* a different colour."

Piglet began to say that this was because he had just had a bath, and then he thought that perhaps he wouldn't say that, and as he opened his mouth to say something else, Kanga slipped the medicine spoon in, and then patted him on the back and told him that it was really quite a nice taste when you got used to it.

"I knew it wasn't Piglet," said Kanga. "I wonder who it can be."

"Perhaps it's some relation of Pooh's," said Christopher Robin. "What about a nephew or an uncle or something?"

Kanga agreed that this was probably what it was, and said that they would have to call it by some name.

"I shall call it Pootel," said Christopher Robin. "Henry Pootel for short."

And just when it was decided, Henry Pootel wriggled out of Kanga's arms and jumped to the ground. To his great joy Christopher Robin had left the door open. Never had Henry Pootel

 Piglet run so fast as he ran then, and he didn't stop running until he had got quite close to his house. But when he was a hundred yards away he stopped running, and rolled the rest of the way home, so as to get his own nice comfortable colour again. . . .

So Kanga and Roo stayed in the Forest. And every Tuesday Roo spent the day with his great friend Rabbit, and every Tuesday Kanga spent the day with her great friend Pooh, teaching him to jump, and every Tuesday Piglet spent the day with his great friend Christopher Robin. So they were all happy again.

Very Important Someone: A. A. Milne

In which Mr. Milne is discovered to have been a highly successful dramatist and humorist before he was the writer of Winnie-the-Pooh; *how and why he wrote what he did; and how Pooh wasn't that impressed by the books of verses.*

From A. A. Milne, *New York Herald Tribune Book Review,* October 12, 1952:

A. A. MILNE—ALWAYS TIME FOR A RHYME

Born in 1892:
(Small, of course, but slowly grew)
Educated, so to say,
In the customary way—
School and college: at the latter
Wrote as madly as a hatter,
Wrote, and used to wonder "Can't a

Man who runs the Cambridge *Granta*
Satisfy for life his creditors
By cajoling London editors?"

A. A. Milne

So to London, and collected
Diverse forms for the rejected;
£20 the year's reward,
Not enough for bed and board.
Two more years went lightly by
Editors still rather shy.
Punch, however, kept its head,
Made me its Assistant Ed.

There I stayed until the War . . .
(Married Her the year before).

Training in the Isle of Wight
Had a little time to Write;
Wrote a play which got a laugh
From my so much better half
(Reason One: Why Men Should Marry):
Sent the play to J. M. Barrie.
Barrie was approving, so
On it went to Boucicault;
And in the ensuing summer he
Staged it (title: *Wurzel Flummery*):
Which, because it wasn't hissed
Changed me to a dramatist . . .

Found, and no one more surprised,
War could end. Demobilized.
Peaceful days succeeded days
Mostly spent creating plays.
Wife's supreme creation, son,
Took the stage in '21.
(That's poetic license, I'm
Hampered by the need for rhyme,
And by "21" I meant he
First appeared in 1920.)
If a writer, why not write
On whatever comes in sight?
So—the Children's Books, a short
Intermezzo of a sort:

When I wrote them, little thinking
All my years of pen-and-inking
Would be almost lost among
Those four trifles for the young.

Though a writer must confess his
Works aren't all of them successes,
Though his sermons fail to please,
Though his humour on one sees,
Yet he cannot help delighting
In the pleasure of the writing.
In a farmhouse old by centuries
This so happy an adventure is
Coming (so I must suppose,
Now I'm 70) to a close.
Take it all, Year In, Year Out,
I've enjoyed it, not a doubt.

A. A. Milne married Dorothy de Selincourt in 1913. She was called Daphne by nearly everybody, and it was she who gave added voice to the toy animals of Christopher Milne.

From *Winnie-the-Pooh,*
dedication to Daphne Milne:

TO HER

Hand in hand we come
Christopher Robin and I

To lay this book in your lap.
Say you're surprised?
Say you like it?
Say it's just what you wanted?
Because it's yours—
Because we love you

From *The House At Pooh Corner*,
dedication to Daphne Milne:

You gave me Christopher Robin, and then
you breathed new life in Pooh.
Whatever of each has left my pen
Goes homing back to you.
My book is ready, and comes to greet
The mother it longs to see—
It would be my present to you, my sweet,
If it weren't your gift to me.

From Dorothy Parker, reviewing as
"Constant Reader," *The New Yorker*, October 20, 1928:

"The more it
SNOWS-*tiddely-pom,*
The more it
GOES-*tiddely-pom*
The more it
GOES-*tiddely-pom*
On
Snowing.

"And nobody
KNOWS-*tiddely-pom,*
How cold my
TOES-*tiddely-pom*
How cold my
TOES-*tiddely-pom*
Are
Growing."

The above lyric is culled from the fifth page of Mr. A. A. Milne's new book, "The House at Pooh Corner," for, although the work is in prose, there are frequent droppings into more cadenced whimsy. This one is designated as a "Hum," that pops into the head of Winnie-the-Pooh as he is standing outside Piglet's house in the snow, jumping up and down to keep warm. It "seemed to him a Good Hum, such as is Hummed Hopefully to Others." In fact, so Good a Hum did it seem that he and Piglet started right out through the snow to Hum It Hopefully to Eeyore. Oh, darn—there I've gone and given away the plot. Oh, I could bite my tongue out.

As they are trotting along against the flakes, Piglet begins to weaken a bit. " 'Pooh,' he said at last, and a little timidly, because he didn't want Pooh to think he was Giving In, 'I was just wondering. How would it be if we went home now and *practised* your song, and then sang it to Eeyore tomorrow—or—or the next day, when we happen to see him.'

" 'That's a very good idea, Piglet,' said Pooh. 'We'll practise it now as we go along. But it's no good going home to practise it, because it's a special Outdoor Song which Has To Be Sung In The Snow.'

" 'Are you sure?' asked Piglet anxiously.

" 'Well, you'll see, Piglet, when you listen. Because this is how it begins. *The more it snows, tiddely-pom*—'

" 'Tiddely what?' said Piglet." (He took, as you might say, the very words out of your correspondent's mouth.)

" 'Pom,' said Pooh. 'I put that in to make it more hummy.' "

And it is that word "hummy," my darlings, that marks the first place in "The House at Pooh Corner" at which Tonstant Weader fwowed up.

From A. A. Milne, *Autobiography:*

In August of that year my collaborator produced a more personal work. We had intended to call it *Rosemary,* but decided later that *Billy* would be more suitable. However, as you can't be christened William—at least, we didn't see why anybody should—we had to think of two other names, two initials being necessary to ensure him any sort of copyright in a cognomen as often plagiarized as Milne. One of us thought of Robin, the other of Christopher; names wasted on him who called himself Billy Moon as soon as he could talk, and has been Moon to his family and friends ever since. I mention this because it explains why the publicity which came to be attached to 'Christopher Robin' never seemed to affect us personally, but to concern either a character in a book or a horse which we hoped at one time would win the Derby.

When he was three, we took a house in North Wales for August with the Nigel Playfairs. It rained continuously. In

the one living-room every morning there were assembled Five Playfairs, Three Milnes, Grace Lovat-Fraser, Joan Pitt-Chatham, Frederic Austin, and a selection of people to whom Nigel had issued casual invitations in London before starting north for what he supposed to be his Welsh castle. In a week I was screaming with agoraphobia. Somehow I must escape. I pleaded urgent inspiration, took a pencil and an exercise-book and escaped to the summer-house. It contained a chair and a table. I sat down on the chair, put my exercise-book on the table, and gazed ecstatically at a wall of mist which might have been hiding Snowdon or the Serpentine for all I saw or cared. I was alone. . . .

But sooner or later I should be asked what I was writing. What was I writing?

About six months earlier, while at work on a play, I had wasted a morning in writing a poem called 'Vespers.' I gave it to Daphne, as one might give a photograph or a valentine, telling her that if she liked to get it published anywhere she could stick to the money. She sent it to Frank Crowninshield of *Vanity Fair* (N.Y.) and got fifty dollars. Later she lent it to me for the Queen's Doll's House Library, and later still collected one-forty-fourth of all the royalties of *When We Were Very Young,* together with her share of various musical and subsidiary rights. It turned out to be the most expensive present I had ever given her. A few months after this, Rose Fyleman was starting a magazine for children. She asked me, I have no idea why, to write some verses for it. I said that I didn't and couldn't, it wasn't in my line. As soon as I had

Christopher Robin and A. A. Milne

posted my letter, I did what I always do after refusing to write anything: wondered how I would have written it if I hadn't refused. One might, for instance, have written:

> *There once was a Dormouse who lived in a bed*
> *Of delphiniums (blue) and geraniums (red),*
> *And all the day long he'd a wonderful view*
> *Of geraniums (red) and delphiniums (blue).*

After another wasted morning I wrote to Miss Fyleman to say that perhaps after all I might write her some verses. A poem called *The Dormouse and the Doctor* was the result. It was illustrated by Harry Rountree; proofs had come to me in Wales; and with them came letters from both illustrator and editor saying: 'Why don't you write a whole book of verses like these?'

So there I was with an exercise-book and pencil, and a fixed determination not to leave the heavenly solitude of that summer-house until it stopped raining . . . and there in London were two people telling me what to write . . . and there on the other side of the lawn was a child with whom I had lived for three years . . . and here within me were unforgettable memories of my own childhood . . . what was I writing? A child's book of verses obviously. Not a whole book, of course; but to write a few would be fun—until I was tired of it. Besides, my pencil had an india-rubber at the back; just the thing for poetry.

I had eleven wet days in that summer-house and wrote eleven sets of verses. Then we went back to London. A little apologetically: feeling that this wasn't really work: feeling that a man of stronger character would be writing that detective-story and making £2,000 for the family: a little as if I were slipping off to Lord's in the morning, or lying in a deck-chair at Osborne reading a novel, I went on writing verses. By the end of the year I had written enough for a book. . . .

It is inevitable that a book which has had very large sales should become an object of derision to critics and columnists. We all write books, we all want money; we who write want money from our books. If we fail to get money, we are not so humble, nor so foolish, as to admit that we have failed in our object. Our object, we maintain, was artistic success. It is easy to convince ourselves that the financial failure of the book is no proof of its artistic failure; and it is a short step from there to affirm that artistic success is, in fact, incompatible with financial success. It must be so: for how else could we be the artists we are and remain in our first editions? If any other artist goes into twenty editions, then he is a traitor to the cause, and we shall hasten to say that he is not one of Us.

All this is commonplace. What has been particularly irritating about the sales of the Christopher Robin books (even though the irritation has produced no more intimidating retort than the writing of the name 'Kwistopher Wobin') is that the books were written for children. When, for instance, Dorothy Parker, as 'Constant Reader' in *The New Yorker,* delights the sophisticated by announcing that at page 5 of *The House at Pooh Corner* 'Tonstant Weader fwowed up' (*sic*, if I may), she leaves the book, oddly enough, much where it was.

However greatly indebted to Mrs Parker, no Alderney, at the approach of the milkmaid, thinks 'I hope this lot will turn out to be gin,' no writer of children's books says gaily to his publisher, 'Don't bother about the children, Mrs Parker will love it.' As an artist one might genuinely prefer that one's novel should be praised by a single critic, whose opinion one valued, rather than be bought by 'the mob'; but there is no artistic reward for a book written for children other than the knowledge that they enjoy it. . . .

Winnie-the-Pooh was written two years later, and it was followed by a second book of verses and, in 1928, *The House at Pooh Corner*. The animals in the stories came for the most part from the nursery. My collaborator had already given them individual voices, their owner by constant affection had given them the twist in their features which denoted character, and Shepard drew them, as one might say, from the living model. They were what they are for anyone to see; I described rather than invented them. Only Rabbit and Owl were my own unaided work. These books also became popular. One day when Daphne went up to the nursery, Pooh was missing from the dinner-table which he always graced. She asked where he was. 'Behind the ottoman,' replied his owner coldly. 'Face downwards. He said he didn't like *When We Were Very Young*.' Pooh's jealousy was natural. He could never quite catch up with the verses.

A. A. Milne's autobiography, aptly called Autobiography, *is a largish book (over 300 pages), and yet only* eight *or so are given over to talk of Pooh's stories or verses. The success of* Winnie-the-Pooh *put him in a bit of a bind. For while it brought him fame, it was only a different fame from that which he already possessed. Where before he was a recognized essayist, dramatist, and wit, he was now a children's writer, and his new public wanted not more adult whimsy but more Bear! And ever afterward, no matter how hard he tried, Mr. Milne was always regarded as the author of the Pooh stories. A. A. Milne died in 1956.*

From A. A. Milne, *Autobiography:*

YOUNG FRIEND: And to what, sir, do you attribute your success?

The famous photograph by Howard Coster of A. A. Milne, Christopher Robin, and Pooh. The original hangs in the National Portrait Gallery in London.

AUTHOR: Don't call me 'sir.' I hate being called 'sir.' I'm not as old as all that.

YOUNG FRIEND: Sorry. And to what—if you'd just get your back to the light . . . and I think a hat . . . thank you—And to what, young man, do you attribute your success?

AUTHOR: Meaning by 'success'?

YOUNG FRIEND: Anything you like. The fact that I bought your last book—I mean got it from the library—I mean it's on my list—dammit, you know quite well what I mean.

AUTHOR: Well, as long as it's clear that I don't mean more than you do.

YOUNG FRIEND: That's all right. You see, what I think you ought to give us now—last chapter and all that—is Something for the Little Ones. A few Helpful Words on Speech Day. Advice to Young Man about to make his way in World. Sum it all up. What's the secret?

AUTHOR: There's only one rule.

YOUNG FRIEND: Well?

AUTHOR: *Never take advice.* Of all sad words of tongue or pen the saddest are 'Why did I listen to Tomkins?'

YOUNG FRIEND: That doesn't rhyme.

AUTHOR: If his name were Benjamin it would.

YOUNG FRIEND: But do you really mean it?

AUTHOR: Absolutely.

YOUNG FRIEND: And that's why you're where you are?

AUTHOR: Wherever that is—yes.

YOUNG FRIEND: How do you know you wouldn't have

been much more successful if you had followed other people's advice?

AUTHOR: I don't. But you didn't ask me to what I attributed my failure.

YOUNG FRIEND: In other words you've always done what you wanted to do, and haven't listened to other people?

AUTHOR: In other words I've listened to other people, and then tried to do what I wanted to do.

YOUNG FRIEND: Which wasn't what *they* wanted you to do?

AUTHOR: Not as a rule.

YOUNG FRIEND: And that's your advice to young authors—young men generally.

AUTHOR: Yes.

YOUNG FRIEND *(after profound thought):* You do see, don't you, that if they take your advice, then they *won't* take your advice, which means that they *will* take advice, which means that—this is getting difficult.

AUTHOR: I know. It's a difficult world.

YOUNG FRIEND: Oh, yes, that reminds me. Oughtn't you to tell us how much more difficult Life has become since you were a boy? Something about the leisurely ease of The Good Old Days. *Laus temporis acti* and all that.

AUTHOR: Well, for one thing we didn't pronounce it like that in the good old days.

YOUNG FRIEND: Splendid. Anything else you've noticed?

AUTHOR: Well—

YOUNG FRIEND: Come on, this is the last chapter. Tell us What You Believe, or What's Wrong with the World, or something.

From *Winnie-the-Pooh:*

... Pooh and Piglet walked home thoughtfully together in the golden evening, and for a long time they were silent.

"When you wake up in the morning, Pooh," said Piglet at last, "what's the first thing you say to yourself?"

"What's for breakfast?" said Pooh. "What do *you* say, Piglet?"

"I say, I wonder what's going to happen exciting *today?*" said Piglet.

Pooh nodded thoughtfully.

"It's the same thing," he said.

Very Important Someone Else: Ernest H. Shepard

In which Ernest H. Shepard tells us something of himself; we discover that he was called Kip or Kipper; and A. A. Milne tells us something about how Mr. E. H. Shepard got to illustrate the Pooh stories.

From A. A. Milne, *By Way of Introduction:*

INTRODUCING SHEPARD

Mr. E. H. Shepard, of all people, needs no introduction at my hands. Anybody who has heard of me has certainly heard of Shepard. Indeed, our names have been associated on so many title-pages that I am beginning to wonder which of us is which. Years ago when I used to write for the paper of whose staff he is now such a decorative member I was continually being asked by strangers if I also drew the cartoons. Sometimes I said 'Yes.' No doubt Mr. Shepard is often asked

137

Ernest H. Shepard

if he wrote 'The King's Breakfast.' I should be proud if he admitted now and then that he did.

. . . We have a perfectly true story in our family that one of us was approached by an earnest woman at some special function with the words, 'Oh, are you the brother of A. J. Milne—or am I thinking of Shepperson?' E. H. Shepard, though surely he owes something to that beautiful draughtsman, is not to be mistaken for Claude Shepperson, nor am I that other, to me unknown, from whom I have so lamentably failed to profit; but you see what she meant. You see also what I mean; and how I am hampered by the fear that somebody may read this Introduction, and feel that Mr. Shepard is not being very modest about himself. For if I let myself go I could make him seem very immodest indeed.

Perhaps this will be a good place in which to tell the story of how I discovered him. It is short, but interesting. In those early days before the war, when he was making his first tentative pictures for *Punch,* I used to say to F. H. Townsend, the Art Editor, on the occasion of each new Shepard drawing, 'What on earth do you see in this man? He's perfectly hopeless,' and Townsend would say complacently, 'You wait.' So I waited. That is the end of the story, which is shorter and less interesting than I thought it was going to be. For it looks now as if the discovery had been somebody else's. Were those early drawings included in this book, we should know definitely whether Townsend was a man of remarkable insight, or whether I was just an ordinary fool. In their absence we may assume fairly safely that he was something of the one, and I more than a little of the other. . . .

Mr. Shepard has the initials E. H., which are short for Ernest H., and he was known to his friends as Kipper or Kip. Born on December 10, 1879, he got the nickname during his teenage years from the then-current and popular music-hall song "Giddy Kipper," which must say something about him, or perhaps not. . . .

From *The Listener,* September 10, 1970:

E. H. SHEPARD, ILLUSTRATOR OF 'WINNIE THE POOH', NOW IN HIS NINETIES, TALKS TO PATRICK HARVEY.

Here you live, Mr Shepard, in the middle of a countryside where I almost expect to see Roo or Kanga or Winnie-the-Pooh himself turning up just about as often as the pheasants I've been seeing this morning. Did they come from these parts?

No. You see, Milne lived at the other end of Sussex and the playground for his little characters was Ashdown Forest close to his farm home. And that is where he took me to see the Hundred Acre Wood and all these places where things really happened. I did most of the background drawings there; I did a few near my home where I used to live in Guildford, where there are some very beautiful trees.

Christopher Robin, when I first knew him, was a little boy of six years old.

Did you discuss the animals with him?

No, I didn't really. I saw the toys—that was the background of it really. But I never saw their Teddy Bear. I drew what had been my own son's Teddy Bear when he was a little boy. He was a lovely Teddy Bear, we called him Growler, and although he lost his growl he remained an entity until he was finally destroyed in Canada. A dog chewed him, worried him.

Which are your own favourites?

My favourites? Eeyore. I have such sympathy for Eeyore always. Dear Eeyore, he was a grand fellow, and of course Piglet was too. When I told Alan Milne that my Pooh Bear had been killed in Canada by a dog he told me that Piglet suffered the same fate in England.

Ernest H. Shepard at his home in Sussex, England, in 1971

I think you suggested just now that some of the settings are exact, that Milne knew exactly where each adventure took place.

Oh, yes. I made a map at the end, an entirely fictitious map really, but giving the names of all the places that he'd mentioned, and most of them he showed me himself.

Later on, when you came to illustrate 'The Wind in the Willows', you were following the same pattern of going to the exact location?

The exact location. Kenneth Grahame himself showed me exactly where to go. When I showed him the sketches I'd made for his book he told me to go to the flat meadows further up, where I should find the sites of where Rat's supposed to have had his little boathouse and his little blue boat, where Mole had lived on the opposite side of the river, and where Otter would swim across with the bubbles showing. . . .

Before you approached illustrating any of these books, you were already established as a member of the 'Punch' Round Table.

Yes, I joined the *Punch* Table in 1921, soon after I came back from the First World War. We used to talk about all sorts of subjects: chiefly the idea was to arrange the cartoons for the following week. We had very good lunches—dinners, I should say. Lunches were later, when the Second War developed. One thing we all had to do was to carve our initials on the table. You'll find on that table the initials of all the members of the *Punch* staff. . . . *Punch* invited me to lunch on my 90th birthday, but as we had already been booked at the Garrick Club, I had to refuse.

About that time, I think you were reminded of your service in the Army.

Yes, I had a greetings telegram from the Master Gunner. That's the proudest thing I could possibly have received, that I should be remembered by the Gunners that I served in the First World War.

Artists aren't usually thought to make good soldiers. Were you a good soldier?

I think I must have been fairly good. If there was a difficult shoot to be done, what you call a close shoot, when there was a raid on and we had to make a curtain of fire round a certain sector, they always asked for one of us to carry it out since we had such a good reputation for shooting. . . .

What puzzles me slightly is that here you were, an artist, presumably no technician, and yet you chose, when you decided to go to war, to go to the Gunners.

Because I always loved guns. As a small boy I had two loves, two ambitions: to be a soldier and to be an artist. And the artist won in the end.

Mr. Shepard's son, Graham, died serving with the British navy during World War II. Mr. Shepard died on March 24, 1976, after a lifetime of drawing and art. In fact, he had been drawing from a very early age, and his only other child, daughter Mary, herself became an artist. She went on to illustrate the Mary Poppins books.

From *Punch,* October 24, 1928:

One of the privileges (and they are many) of a lack of high seriousness in writing is the condition of static youth with which you are able to endow your characters. King Pandion he is dead, dust hath closed Helen's eyes, but *Pickwick, Tartarin* and *Winnie-the-Pooh* go on for ever. If only Mr A. A. MILNE had made *Christopher Robin* a less integral part of the *Pooh* epic, we could have had *Pooh, Eeyore, Rabbit, Kanga, Roo* and the rest of them here for an eternity of Christmases. But *Christopher Robin,* "bearing," as ST. AUGUSTINE would say, "his mortality about with him," was always the Achilles' heel of the confederacy, and, when midway through *The House at Pooh Corner* (METHUEN), *Christopher Robin* began having lessons in the morning, we all of us—*Pooh, Eeyore, Rabbit, Kanga, Roo* and myself—knew it was the beginning of the end. Of course it is a very captivating end. *Pooh,* still addicted to a little smackerel of something at eleven, is the same astute and helpful bear; *Rabbit* is even more captainish;

Eeyore, the rarest to my mind of Mr Milne's creations, has better lines than ever; and a new denizen of the forest, the strange and bouncey *Tigger,* brings an element of modern unrest into the lives of the older established. If I cannot vow with my hand on my heart that the last book is better than the first, I can at last swear it is as good; and that—I have the whole nursery behind me—is good enough for anybody. As for Mr Shepard's pictures, they recapture all our old friends, with the wind and water, trees and bracken, snug little homes and frosty little expeditions that belong to them, as only Mr Shepard's pictures can.

And what is it that Mr. Shepard's decorations have captured? Somehow Mr. Shepard's pencil knew what Pooh was all about. It may have been the placing of the eye in that just right position (as Christopher Robin maintains) that did it, or it could be the special way Pooh's ears seem always pulled back as if he is continually amazed. Whatever! Mr. Shepard caught Pooh's poohing nature, just as Mr. Milne had so keenly described it in the hum "NOISE, BY POOH":

> *Oh, the honey-bees are gumming*
> *On their little wings, and humming*
> *That the summer, which is coming,*
> > *Will be fun.*
>
> *And the cows are almost cooing,*
> *And the turtle-doves are mooing,*
> *Which is why a Pooh is poohing*
> > *In the sun.*

Whatever debates historians, literary critics, art critics, art historians, letter-writers, and other what-nots may stir up concerning which bear was which as the original model of Mr. Shepard's decorations, the definitive Pooh was revealed by Mr. Shepard.

Afterwords and Other Things

And so we come to the end. But we don't say good-bye. Not ever. In only two small books the complete world of Pooh was laid out, and in that world each and every reader is invited to stay or just visit.

From its publication in 1926, Winnie-the-Pooh *has remained a best-seller. The appearance of* The House At Pooh Corner *two years later only confirmed what some early critics rightly knew. There is no Bear like Winnie-the-Pooh.*

From *The New York Times,* November 11, 1928:

WINNIE-THE-POOH IS BACK AGAIN!
THE HOUSE AT POOH CORNER
By A. A. Milne. With Decorations by Ernest H. Shepard.
178 pp. New York: E. P. Dutton & Co. $2.

The first thing the children will want to be sure about in
146   this sequel to Winnie-the-Pooh is that it is actually about

Pooh Bear, Piglet, Eeyore, Rabbit, Roo and the other remarkable characters in Christopher Robin's play world.
They will be immediately reassured by the first sentence,
which begins, as might be expected, with the assertion that
"One day when Pooh Bear had nothing else to do, he thought
he would do something." This, as every child knows, is true
Milne. The young readers or listeners—for Milne is emi-
nently an author to be read aloud—will sink back content-
edly to learn how Pooh Bear and Piglet built Eeyore, as they
supposed, a new house. They will hear how Tigger, a brand
new Strange Animal, had trouble finding just the diet that
suited him. Honey wouldn't do, and neither would haycorns,
and neither would thistles. It turned out that what he needed
and wanted was Roo's Extract of Malt. They will be told how
Piglet and Pooh went hunting for Small, though they weren't
sure quite what Small was, and how they fell into a piece of
the forest which had been left out by mistake. They will be
apprised of how the Tigger got up in a tree, was mistaken for
a Jagular and had a terrible time being rescued. They will be
informed of how Eeyore was bounced into the river and how
he got out, and of how Rabbit, Piglet and Pooh tried to make
the Tigger a little less Bouncy. They will be dreadfully
alarmed when Owl's tree blows down, but reassured when
Piglet escapes through the letter box, and doubly reassured
when the Owl, with Christopher Robin's help, finds a new
house. If this new house turns out to be Piglet's, it gives Piglet
a chance to be noble, and every child knows how much fun it
is to be noble. Finally, sad to relate, Christopher Robin has to
go away. Perhaps he grows up. "But," as every reader will be

glad to know, "wherever they go, and whatever happens to them on the way, in that enchanted place on the top of the Forest, a little boy and his Bear will always be playing."

There the story ends for its childish auditors. Strangely enough, even the adults who have been amusing the children by reading it aloud lay it down with a sigh of regret. A. A. Milne's fun is of a sort that is especially at home in a children's book. But every good children's book has something in it for adults, since children, to all intents and purposes, are adults. In Piglet, in Pooh Bear, and especially in Eeyore, Milne has created characters that, with very little dressing-up, might be carried over into adult fiction. The world in miniature moves through Christopher Robin's forest—is, in fact, Christopher Robin's forest. When Christopher Robin grows up and recurs to the adventures of his childhood, he will find that a number of things have not changed and that the motivations of his infancy are also those in large measure of his grown-up life.

It is hard to tell what Pooh Bear and his friends would have been without the able assistance of Ernest H. Shepard to see them and picture them so cleverly. Shepard and Milne are as indispensable one to the other as Sir John Tenniel and Lewis Carroll. The highest praise one can give them is that they do not in this book fall appreciably below the level of Winnie-the-Pooh. They are, and should be, classics.

The best thing about a book is that the story ends, but not the reading. A good book is to be read over and over until the joy so freely given by the author becomes our own joy. The stories of

Pooh, of Piglet, of Eeyore (and of Rabbit, Owl, Kanga, Roo, Tigger, and Christopher Robin) have quickly become the stories of childhood. And if the stories are anything, they are of simple things and grand laughter. They are the stories of Everyone.

From *The House At Pooh Corner:*

CHRISTOPHER ROBIN AND POOH COME TO AN
ENCHANTED PLACE, AND WE LEAVE THEM THERE

Christopher Robin was going away. Nobody knew why he was going; nobody knew where he was going; indeed, nobody even knew why he knew that Christopher Robin *was* going away. But somehow or other everybody in the Forest felt that it was happening at last. Even Smallest-of-All, a friend-and-relation of Rabbit's who thought he had once seen Christopher Robin's foot, but couldn't be sure because perhaps it was something else, even S.-of-A. told himself that Things were going to be Different; and Late and Early, two other friends-and-relations, said, "Well, Early?" and "Well, Late?" to each other in such a hopeless sort of way that it really didn't seem any good waiting for the answer.

One day when he felt that he couldn't wait any longer, Rabbit brained out a Notice, and this is what it said:

"Notice a meeting of everybody will meet at the House at Pooh Corner to pass a Rissolution By Order Keep to the Left Signed Rabbit."

He had to write this out two or three times before he could get the rissolution to look like what he thought it was going to when he began to spell it: but, when at last it was finished, he took it round to everybody and read it out to them. And they all said they would come.

"Well," said Eeyore that afternoon, when he saw them all walking up to his house, "this *is* a surprise. Am *I* asked too?"

"Don't mind Eeyore," whispered Rabbit to Pooh. "I told him all about it this morning."

Everybody said "How-do-you-do" to Eeyore, and Eeyore said that he didn't, not to notice, and then they sat down; and as soon as they were all sitting down, Rabbit stood up again.

"We all know why we're here," he said, "but I have asked my friend Eeyore—"

"That's Me," said Eeyore. "Grand."

"I have asked him to Propose a Rissolution." And he sat down again. "Now then, Eeyore," he said.

"Don't Bustle me," said Eeyore, getting up slowly. "Don't now-then me." He took a piece of paper from behind his ear, and unfolded it. "Nobody knows anything about this," he went on. "This is a Surprise." He coughed in an important way, and began again: "What-nots and Etceteras, before I begin, or perhaps I should say, before I end, I have a piece of Poetry to read to you. Hitherto—hitherto—a long word meaning—well, you'll see what it means directly—hitherto, as I was saying, all the Poetry in the Forest has been written by Pooh, a Bear with a Pleasing Manner but a Positively Startling Lack of Brain. The Poem which I am now about to read to you was written by Eeyore, or Myself, in a Quiet Moment. If somebody will take Roo's bull's-eye away from him, and wake up Owl, we shall all be able to enjoy it. I call it— POEM."

This was it.

Christopher Robin is going.
At least I think he is.
Where?
Nobody knows.
But he is going—
I mean he goes
(To rhyme with "knows")
Do we care?
(To rhyme with "where")
We do
Very much.
(I haven't got a rhyme for that
   "is" in the second line yet.
   Bother.)
(Now I haven't got a rhyme for
   bother. Bother.)
Those two bothers will have
   to rhyme with each other
   Buther.
The fact is this is more difficult
   than I thought,
I ought—
(Very good indeed)
I ought
To begin again,
But it is easier
To stop.
Christopher Robin, good-bye,

I
(Good)
I
And all your friends
Sends—
I mean all your friend
Send—
(Very awkward this, it keeps
   going wrong)
Well, anyhow, we send
   Our love
END.

"If anybody wants to clap," said Eeyore when he had read this, "now is the time to do it."

They all clapped.

"Thank you," said Eeyore. "Unexpected and gratifying, if a little lacking in Smack."

"It's much better than mine," said Pooh admiringly, and he really thought it was.

"Well," explained Eeyore modestly, "it was meant to be."

"The rissolution," said Rabbit, "is that we all sign it, and take it to Christopher Robin."

So it was signed PooH, PIGLET, WOL, EOR, RABBIT, KANGA, BLOT, SMUDGE, and they all went off to Christopher Robin's house with it. "Hallo, everybody," said Christopher Robin—"Hallo, Pooh."

They all said "Hallo," and felt awkward and unhappy suddenly, because it was a sort of good-bye they were saying, and they didn't want to think about it. So they stood around, and waited for somebody else to speak, and they nudged each other, and said "Go on," and gradually Eeyore was nudged to the front, and the others crowded behind him.

"What is it, Eeyore?" asked Christopher Robin. Eeyore swished his tail from side to side, so as to encourage himself, and began.

"Christopher Robin," he said, "we've come to say—to give you—it's called—written by—but we've all—because we've heard, I mean we all know—well, you see, it's—we—you—well, that, to put it as shortly as possible, is what it is." He turned round angrily on the others and said, "Everybody crowds round so in this Forest. There's no Space. I never saw a more Spreading lot of animals in my life, and all in the wrong places. Can't you *see* that Christopher Robin wants to be alone? I'm going." And he humped off.

Not quite knowing why, the others began edging away, and when Christopher Robin had finished reading POEM, and was looking up to say, "Thank you," only Pooh was left.

"It's a comforting sort of thing to have," said Christopher Robin, folding up the paper, and putting it in his pocket. "Come on, Pooh," and he walked off quickly.

"Where are we going?" said Pooh, hurrying after him, and wondering whether it was to be an Explore or a What-shall-I-do-about-you-know-what.

"Nowhere," said Christopher Robin.

So they began going there, and after they had walked a little way Christopher Robin said:

"What do you like doing best in the world, Pooh?"

"Well," said Pooh, "what I like best—" and then he had to stop and think. Because although Eating Honey *was* a very good thing to do, there was a moment just before you began to eat it which was better than when you were, but he didn't know what it was called. And then he thought that being with Christopher Robin was a very good thing to do, and having Piglet near was a very friendly thing to have; and so, when he had thought it all out, he said, "What I like best in the whole world is Me and Piglet going to see You, and You saying, 'What about a little something?' and Me saying, 'Well, I shouldn't mind a little something, should you, Piglet,' and it being a hummy sort of day outside, and birds singing."

"I like that too," said Christopher Robin, "but what I like *doing* best is Nothing."

"How do you do Nothing?" asked Pooh, after he had wondered for a long time.

"Well, it's when people call out at you just as you're going off to do it, What are you going to do, Christopher Robin, and you say, Oh, nothing, and then you go and do it."

"Oh, I see," said Pooh.

"This is a nothing sort of thing that we're doing now."

"Oh, I see," said Pooh again.

"It means just going along, listening to all the things you can't hear, and not bothering."

"Oh!" said Pooh.

From Christopher Milne, *The Enchanted Places:*

In the last chapter of *The House At Pooh Corner* our ways

part. I go on to become a
schoolboy. A child and
his bear remain playing
in the enchanted spot at
the top of the forest.
The toys are left behind,
no longer wanted, in the
nursery. So a glass case
was made for them and
it was fastened to the
nursery wall . . . , and
they climbed inside.
And there they lived,
sometimes glanced at,
mostly forgotten, until
the war came. Roo was
missing. He had been

Christopher Milne

lost years before, in the
apple orchard up the lane. And Piglet's face was a funny
shape where a dog had bitten him. During the war they went
to America and there they have been ever since. . . .

If you saw them today, your immediate reaction would be:
"How old and battered and lifeless they look." But of course
they are old *and* battered *and* lifeless. They are only toys and
you are mistaking them for the real animals who lived in the
forest. Even in their prime they were no more than a first
rough sketch, the merest hint of what they were to become,
and they are now long past their prime. Eeyore is the most
recognizable; Piglet the least. So, if I am asked "Aren't
you sad that the animals are not in their glass case with

you today?" I must answer "Not really," and hope that this doesn't seem too unkind. I like to have around me the things I like today, not the things I once liked many years ago. I don't want a house to be a museum. . . . Every child has his Pooh, but one would think it odd if every man still kept his Pooh to remind him of his childhood. But my Pooh is different, you say: he is *the* Pooh. No, this only makes him different to you, not different to me. My toys were and are to me no more than yours were and are to you. I do not love them more because they are known to children in Australia or Japan. Fame has nothing to do with love.

I wouldn't like a glass case that said: "Here is fame"; and I don't need a glass case to remind me: "Here was love."

Suggested Further Reading

MORE ON A. A. MILNE:

Haring-Smith, Tori. *A. A. Milne: A Critical Biography*. New York: Garland Publishing, 1982.
    For the dedicated Pooh fan, this book cannot be bettered as a guide to printed material on the Pooh books and the Milne family.

Milne, A. A. *By Way of Introduction*. New York: E. P. Dutton, 1929.
    There is nothing here about Pooh, and some of the subject matter and some of the jokes are dated, but the humor and wit are clearly Milne's!

———— *Autobiography*. New York: E. P. Dutton, 1939.

Thwaite, Ann. *A. A. Milne: The Man Behind Winnie-the-Pooh*. New York: Random House, 1990.
    This is a Very Big Book on Milne, and a Very Long Read. Well worth it, however.

————*The Brilliant Career of Winnie-the-Pooh*. New York: Dutton
Children's Books, 1994.

This book's subtitle says it best: *The Definitive History of the Best
Bear in All the World*.

MORE ON CHRISTOPHER MILNE:

Milne, Christopher. *The Enchanted Places*. New York: E. P. Dutton,
1975.

————*The Path Through the Trees*. New York: E. P. Dutton, 1979.

These two autobiographical volumes are intriguing and pleasant
to read. The son writes quite differently from the father—there is
less wit, but a lot more humor. There are flashes of quite personal de-
tail, but there is also a fierce sense of privacy.

————*The Hollow on the Hill*. London: Methuen, 1982.

This is what one might call a small spiritual reflection. A very
good follow-up to the first two books.

MORE ON ERNEST H. SHEPARD:

Knox, Rawle, ed. *The Work of E. H. Shepard*. London: Methuen, 1979.

An edited collection of articles and views on Mr. Shepard as an
artist. It is a serious book, done by friends and admirers, and by the
end of it the reader feels—well, quite warm and friendly toward Mr.
Shepard.

Shepard, Ernest H. *Drawn from Memory*. New York: E. P. Dutton,
1957.

The artist's memories of a single year—1887—of his boyhood.

————*Drawn from Life*. New York: E. P. Dutton, 1962

A second memoir, covering the years 1890-1904: Shepard's adolescence, early adulthood, and first marriage.

Sibley, Brian. *The Pooh Sketchbook*. New York: Dutton, 1982.

A delightful book that shows the magic of Mr. Shepard at work. Many of the Pooh illustrations are shown in the various stages of creation, and there are some new sketches (that is, "new" because the reader has not seen them before).

MORE ON POOH:

Crews, Frederick C. *The Pooh Perplex*. New York: E. P. Dutton, 1965.

The very clever and witty Mr. Crews takes a poke at stuffy academics but never ends up laughing *at* Pooh. Rather, it's Pooh who shows how laughable contemporary literary criticism can be.

Hoff, Benjamin. *The Tao of Pooh*. New York: Dutton, 1982.

Pooh is here, and so is Piglet, and so is a great deal about the Chinese religious and philosophical approach to life that is often called Taoism, or "the Way."

————*The Te of Piglet*. New York: Dutton, 1992.

A follow-up that has a lot less Pooh but a lot more Piglet—and a lot more Taoism. These two books by Hoff should be read as companion pieces.

Melrose, A. R. *The Pooh Dictionary*. New York: Dutton, 1995.

A chatty and humorous guide to how Pooh and all the Animals in the Forest say exactly what they mean.

Williams, John Tyerman. *Pooh and the Philosophers*. New York: Dutton, 1996.

   A light but sufficiently detailed attempt to place Pooh at the center of Western philosophy. Or, perhaps, it is an attempt to show that all of Western philosophy is but a *preparation* for Pooh. It is a work of Ursinian scholarship, in any case.

Index
to This Book

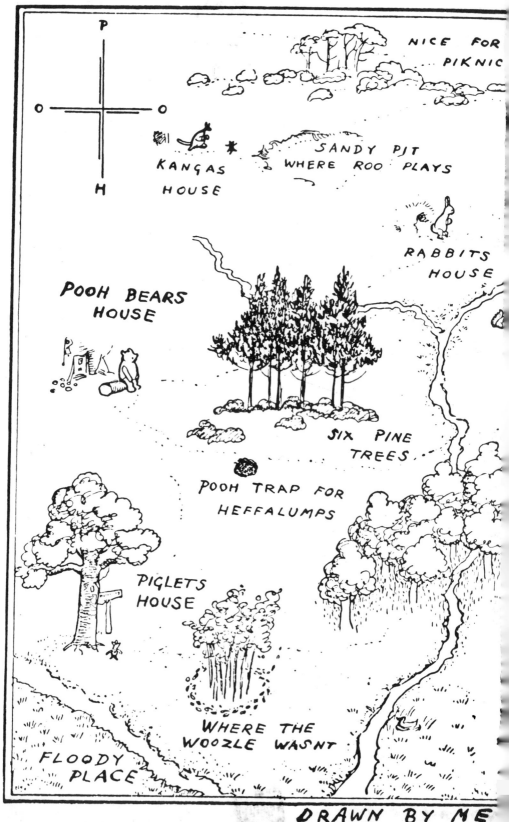